MW00910562

The Detective Company

by
Rich Baldwin
and
Sandie Jones

Illustrated by Dawn Baumer
© Buttonwood Press 2004

ISBN 0-9742920-0-1

Disclaimer

This set of five stories is the product of the imaginations of the authors. These stories have no purpose other than to entertain the reader.

Copyright © 2004 by Rich Baldwin and Sandie Jones All rights reserved. No part of this book may be reproduced or transmitted in any form or by any means, electronic or mechanical, including photocopying, recording, or by any information storage and retrieval system, without permission in writing from the publisher.

Published by

Buttonwood Press, LLC
P.O. Box 716
Haslett, Michigan 48840
www.buttonwoodpress.com

Dedication

The authors of these stories wish
to dedicate this book to their families
of grandchildren:
Ben, Bree, David, Drew, Hannah,
Jack, Katie, Nick, and Tom
and in memory of a very special
little girl named Sharon

Acknowledgments

The authors of this book had a delightful time putting their heads together via the Internet to tell these stories. We extend our thanks to Joyce Wagner, our proofreader; whose sharp eye caught the flaws within. We want to thank Gail Garber and Bree Asher for their suggestions on ways to brighten our stories. Thanks too to Dawn for marvelous illustrations and cover design. Finally we wish to thank our spouses, Patty Baldwin and Bruce Jones, for their love, support and belief in our efforts.

Introduction

The ten middle school students who are members of The Detective Company are purposely named for our two families of grandchildren and one little girl who despite being born with Down's Syndrome, was just one of the inspirations for our fictional cast of characters.

The group has different races represented as well as several of the students have special needs. Despite what one may see as a handicap, each of these children have distinct talents to share in detecting crimes in their own surroundings.

The Case of the
Absent Swimmer

"Brrrrrrrnnngggggggg." As the day's final bell sounded in the hallway, classroom doors burst open. The students of Centerville Middle School scurried with happy voices to their lockers. The doors were banged open and shut as jackets were put on and books shoved into backpacks for the trip home or to after-school activities. In a matter of minutes, the hallway emptied and silence returned once again.

From somewhere in the distance, a soft whirring noise could be heard; whirring and squeaks in the rhythm of footsteps. The sounds increased when suddenly around the corner sped

Maggie McMillan, riding in her battery-powered wheelchair. She was obviously in a hurry. Moving along beside her was Ben, the lead detective in this story, his gym shoes squeaking as he hurried to keep up.

Ben had been with Maggie when the call came in from the Centerville Police Chief. "We've got a case that has us stumped, Maggie. I was wondering if you could assign one of your Detective Company members to give us a hand."

"I'm sure that can be arranged, Chief. What's the problem?"

"This sounds pretty simple, Maggie, but it's got us baffled. We can't seem to figure out why the high school swimming team is losing its meets when they are top swimmers!"

"Do you think a crime is being committed, Chief?" Maggie asked.

"We don't know, but the parents have been suggesting that something illegal may be going on."

"You mean like paying kids not to swim well?"

"No, I don't think that's it, but it may be. We've looked into it and we simply find no clues. I thought one of your young detectives might be

4

able to make sense of it all. Kids often confide things to other kids that they would never tell adults."

"We'll give it a try. I'll bring Ben down to the station and perhaps one of your officers can inform us about what you already know. My guess is you have much more important crimes to solve than why a swimming team is losing its meets."

"Well, every potential illegal activity is of concern to us, but yes, we've got some major problems on our hands and we sure could use your help with this one."

Maggie McMillan is a well known private investigator that serves as the coordinator and mentor of The Detective Company at Centerville Middle School. Ten students make up her band of detectives that meet after school to solve mysteries that occur in their surroundings.

Ben and Maggie hurried down to the Centerville Police Station to be brought up-to-date with the problem. Officer Brink ushered them into a small room and closed the door. This was an enjoyable part of his job, working with one of Maggie's detectives. These young people had been taught to listen carefully, watch with eagle eyes and reason deductively.

Maggie introduced Officer Brink to Ben telling the officer that Ben was the 'bug' man. "I hope that doesn't mean you are bugging people's phones to listen to their conversations," said Officer Brink, looking at Ben out of the corner of his eye and then grinning.

"Oh no, sir. Maggie calls me that because I collect insects," answered Ben, smiling back.

"That sounds like an interesting hobby," Officer Brink said. "Let's see if you can find the insect that is causing so much trouble with the high school swim team."

Opening a file, the officer became serious, "At each meet, one swimmer doesn't show up and they narrowly lose the meet by a few points. First, the breaststroke competitor didn't make the bus, then the next time the free-style swimmer was absent and it simply goes like this meet after meet."

"What do the team members say when they are asked why they were absent?" asked Ben with a frown.

"They have all called the coach, claiming they are sick to their stomachs and vomiting."

"Don't they have a championship team this year?" Maggie asked.

"Yeah, they could be state champs," Ben replied with pride.

"So how long is the swimmer out sick?" asked Maggie.

7

Looking perplexed, Officer Brink consulted his notes and said, "The day after the meet, the absent swimmer shows up for practice and swims like always. A swimmer will miss one meet but this occasionally is enough to tip the meet in favor of the opponent and they win by a point or two."

"Has the star sprinter been absent yet?" Ben asked.

"Oh, you mean Eric Roberts?"

When Ben nodded, the officer said, "Not yet." Maggie and Ben thanked Officer Brink for the briefing, promised to give the case their full attention, and headed back to school.

En route to The Detective Company office, Ben said, "I think we should find a swimmer who hasn't been absent, follow him, and see what develops. The season is winding down and a meet is coming up that would qualify our team for the state finals."

"Do you know the star sprinter you mentioned at the police station?" Maggie asked.

"I know who he is, but I don't think he pays much attention to me. He's a senior. My dad reads me sports page articles about him." Ben has a learning disability and finds reading difficult. Although he cannot read very well, his sharp insight helps him figure out how to solve a crime.

The next day, all members of The Detective Company were given a note by their teacher at the beginning of the day.

TO: The members of the Detective Company

A special meeting of The Detective Company will be held immediately after school today. Please attend if at all possible.

Thanks!

After the members of the club assembled that afternoon, Maggie called the meeting to order. She explained that the reason for the special meeting was to inform the members of a new case that had opened just the day before. "I've assigned Ben to this case involving the high school boys' swim team. Ben, please share the facts in this case, which we'll entitle **The Case of the Absent Swimmer.**

Ben grinned as he stood to share the problem with his fellow detectives. This was his first case and he tried to act as cool as he had seen the other members when giving a report. Following his brief but accurate report, Detective Company members began to voice their thoughts.

10

"Somebody may be putting some poison into the pool," Sharon suggested.

"I don't think so or everybody would get sick at the same time," Ben reasoned.

"Sometimes I get sick when I am worried about something important coming up," Drew thought out loud. "Maybe a swimmer gets nervous about his event and gets sick."

"Possible," Ben replied. "Something is happening to cause them to be sick."

"Maybe these guys are simply passing around a virus," offered Jack.

"That's possible. However, it seems strange that only one gets sick the day of a meet and is better and at practice the next day," Ben replied.

Once the ideas of the Company were exhausted, Ben was on his own to solve the case. Other detectives shared some information about their cases while they snacked and enjoyed a soft drink. The meeting lasted about an hour and once Maggie adjourned the group, the members of The Detective Company set out for home.

Maggie asked Ben to stay a bit longer so she could learn what he was thinking about as first

11

steps to solve the mystery. "I think I'd like to get to know the star sprinter," Ben said.

"Do you need an introduction? One of our senior members at the high school could arrange it."

"No, my family and his family go to the YMCA. I'm sure I can talk to him there."

Maggie called Ben's parents to explain the case and to let them know she would give him a lift home since it was close to the dinner hour.

On Saturday morning, Ben spotted Eric in the men's locker room at the "Y". Taking the locker just adjacent to where Eric was hanging up his jacket, Ben casually put down his duffel bag and sat on the bench facing the lockers. "Hi, Eric," Ben said, looking up and smiling.

"Hey, Ben. How's it goin'?" Eric said as he playfully punched Ben's arm and then sat down

Relieved that Eric knew his name, Ben turned toward the swimmer and said, "Hey, I need to talk to you, Eric."

"No kidding? What gives?"

"I'm working on a problem for The Detective Company and am hoping you can help me."

"Okay, that sounds fun," Eric said, looking interested. "So what do you want with me, pal?"

"I think you can help solve a mystery."

"Who, me? Hey, no way, man," Eric said, looking bored. "Nothing mysterious happens to me. All I do is eat, sleep, do homework and practice at every pool in town."

"Well, give me a chance to tell you how I think you can help us."

"Okay, shoot."

"Well, as you know at most of the swim meets, one excellent swimmer doesn't show up and you guys lose the meet."

"Yeah. Must be some virus going around."

"What if it's a deliberate attempt to keep one of your guys away from the meet?"

"Hey, man, there's a word for that," Eric said looking Ben right in the eye. "Sabotage."

"You're right, but that could be what's happening."

"That's hard to believe, Ben."

"I know, Eric."

"So, how do you think I can help? I haven't been sick."

"That's why I think you are the one who can help us. I need you to keep track of everything you eat for awhile. Everything."

"You want me to write it all down?"

"Yeah, if something goes into your mouth, we need to know it. Okay?"

"Okay, but I hope you're wrong, Ben."

"If I am, you will help rule out the possibility of poisoning. Just keep track of what you eat and if any-thing unusual happens, call me at The Detective Company or at home. Here's my card."

"Okay, Ben, it's a deal. I think your working for The Detective Company is cool," Eric said sincerely. "I wish I had been a member when I was in middle school. It must be exciting, working with the cops and all that stuff."

"Yeah, it's fun, but the best part is solving a

crime. But hey, winning a swim meet is really cool!"

"Yeah, but I'm just trying to be first to arrive at the other end of the pool."

"You're a star, Eric, and our town is proud of you and the team."

"Thanks, Ben. Hey, I'll be in touch," Eric promised. "The state meet is coming up. Maybe you'll have this mystery solved by then."

"I hope so. Thanks, Eric!"

Just two days later, Ben was working on his insect collection. He had gotten up before breakfast to search through his insect book for the bug a friend of his father's had sent to him in a jar. It was a large bug, had lacy wings and was dead. Locating its picture in the book, he carefully opened the lid on the large flat box he and his dad had purchased at the State University bookstore. It was filled with a layer of cotton and had a transparent lid for viewing the bugs that were placed there. Putting the insect on the cotton, Ben began to copy its order and name onto a strip of paper -- *Auchenorrhyncha: Cicada* -- when the phone rang.   His mother answered and said, "Just a minute, please. Ben, it's for you."

Taking the basement stairs two steps at a time, Ben picked up the phone. "Hello."

"Ben? This is Eric."

"What's up?"

"Can you meet me right away in front of the high school? I know it's early but I need to talk to you in private."

"I'll leave right away."

"Thanks, Ben."

"I'll be back in a few minutes, Mom. This may be a clue for the Detective Company," Ben called to his mother as he dashed out the door.

As Ben rode his bicycle toward the high school, more than an hour before school opened, he felt an excitement building inside him. He hoped that Eric would have information to help solve the case. He spotted Eric leaning against the building, a worried look on his face.

"Hi, Eric. Are you okay?"

"Listen, Ben, something happened yesterday

16

that I can't share with my parents or my coach."

"But you're willing to share it with me?"

"Well, I promised you and I won't let you down. But I can't have my parents know or my coach, you understand. Can you keep a secret?"

"Sure, if you trust me, I can keep a secret."

"Well, some kid I don't know came up to me at lunch yesterday. He said that for a buck, he had some stuff that would give me an edge in today's meet. He said that if I took it right after breakfast before a meet, it would give me an edge to win."

"You didn't take it; did you, Eric?"

"Not yet, but he sounded like he knew what he was talking about, Ben."

"I definitely want to win this meet tonight," Eric continued. "We'll be sprinting against one of the state's best swim relay teams. The guy said it wasn't illegal, just something that would give me an edge."

"I wish you wouldn't take it, Eric." Ben said with deep concern in his voice, "I'm afraid you'll get sick like the others."

"Don't worry, Ben. I'll be okay and I'll win my event anyway."

"Who gave it to you, Eric?"

"I don't know the guy. But thinking about it, I realize that I could get into trouble for taking something to enhance my swimming. Plus the guy made it clear that he didn't want anyone finding out about him."

"Okay, Eric, but tell me, is he a high school student?"

"Yeah. I think so."

"When did he give it to you?" asked Ben.

"During lunch period yesterday. He saw me alone for a few seconds and came up to me."

"And you don't know who he is?"

"Never saw him before but we've got a big

school. Please Ben, don't tell anyone."

"I'll keep my promise. Thanks for keeping yours!"

As Ben put on his brakes to turn into the driveway, he spotted his father standing in the driveway holding his briefcase.

"Stop for a moment, son," his father said.

Stopping his bike at his father's side, Ben let his one foot rest on the ground. "What is it, Dad?"

"Let's go to the swim meet tonight, Ben. Perhaps that would help you solve the case you are working on."

"Oh, thanks, Dad! That will be great."

Watching his father back out of the garage, he waved and they smiled at each other.

Eating his breakfast, Ben could not keep his enthusiasm from showing as he chatted with his mother, bringing her up-to-date. "I hope I can solve this case, Mom. I never thought that working on something could be so exciting."

That night, Ben and his father entered the Natatorium at the Centerville High School and climbed the stairs to the spectators' stands. His father had told him to wear a short-sleeved shirt as the huge room was kept very warm for the benefit of the swimmers.

As the team filed in tunelessly chanting the fight song of the school, the excitement began to build among the crowd. All the team members looked similar in the sweat suits they wore over their swim trunks.

Ben looked at each team member closely trying to spot Eric. Being above the team and about thirty yards from them, it was hard to recognize faces. Some team members had shaved heads, the others all wore tight swim caps to gain a second or two of speed when in the water.

The swim meet was exciting as the Centerville swimmers showed their prowess and skills more often than not taking first place in their event. The crowd showed their enthusiasm with clapping and cheering.

As each event was held, Ben could still not pinpoint which swimmer was Eric. Turning to his

20

father, Ben asked, "Dad, can you see Eric?"

When his father shook his head, the man sitting behind Eric, leaned forward and shouted above the din, "I don't see Eric either. I wonder if he is here."

The final event was always the relay and Ben leaned forward in his seat as the team stood in a line awaiting the start of the race. Ben knew that Eric would be the final swimmer in the event.

Centerville was in the lead moving along neck and neck with another team when the last swimmers dove into the pool. In the excitement, the home team had brought the crowd to their feet and the din of encouraging spectators had reached a roar.

Ben knew the Centerville swimmer was not Eric when the other team shot ahead into the lead. If it was Eric, he should have at least kept up with the other swimmer. Now Ben wondered if Eric had indeed taken the substance that he had been sold and was feeling too sick to keep up.

As that last Centerville swimmer reached the pool's edge in second place, he quickly lifted himself from the pool and got consoling pats from

21

his team mates. He pulled off his cap and his curly blond hair proved to Ben that the swimmer was not Eric. With a sigh, Ben sat down disappointed.

"Hey, Ben. Don't look so glum. It was a great meet. Centerville took first place despite coming in second for two events."

"We should have won that last event, Dad," Ben explained. "Eric did not show up and that means we still could lose in the state finals due to an absent swimmer.

"Ah, this is additional evidence for your mystery," Ben's father said as he put his arm around his son. "I'm sure you will think of a way to solve this case. I'm proud of you, Ben."

The next morning, Ben called Maggie at home. He told her about attending the swim meet the night before and then said, "I've got a problem."

"You're supposed to come up with solutions to problems, not have problems," Maggie said with a twinge of humor. "Seriously, what's the problem?"

"Well, I guess I can't even tell you the problem."

"Oh, my! My investigator can't tell the head of the Detective Company the problem?"

"Nope. I promised someone I'd keep what I heard to myself, but I can't solve the problem without squealing."

"Oh, you gave your word to a source, I take it."

"Yeah, I did."

"Well, this will challenge your skills, Ben."

"Yes, it will. In fact, I just had an idea."

"You're good with ideas, Ben."

"Sorry to bother you, Maggie. I think I know how I can keep my promise and solve this crime."

"You don't have to apologize, sometimes talking about something will trigger a solution. Glad I could help by only listening. Good luck."

Ben looked at his notes and discovered that the only other star swimmer who had not missed a meet was Rex Horvath, the last swimmer in the individual medley. Ben also assumed that each swimmer given the drug probably received it at lunch the day before a meet. The next meet was four days away.

Monday morning, Ben shared his plan with Maggie who contacted the high school principal to clear his coming to the high school the day before the final swimming meet. Ben would cover Rex Horvath like a glove, take notes, and perhaps try to snap some photos of anyone who approached him, talked to him, or gave him something. He got permission from Principal White to be absent from the middle school during lunch period.

Ben arrived about eleven-thirty, his tall frame obscuring his age. As he walked into the lunch-room, his eyes locked onto Rex. Ben's heart was racing with excitement as he positioned himself a safe distance away. He unwrapped his turkey sandwich and slowly ate it, watching Rex with nonchalance.

At first, friends gathered around Rex but then left to get into the lunch line. Rex was alone when another student approached. Rex appeared not to recognize the lone student, as he paid little attention to him when he sat down beside him. Within a minute, the student had engaged Rex in a serious discussion. Finally, Rex took out his wallet and gave some money to the guy and in return received a small bottle.

Ben, in the meantime, was snapping photos of the transaction with his high speed film that required no flash. He also was using his sharp powers of observation to note any distinctive features of the guy. Ben didn't think he was a good judge of age, but he wouldn't be surprised if the person talking to Rex was older than a high school student.

Once the transfer took place, Rex and the guy shook hands. Ben quickly took out the cell phone Maggie had loaned him and called the police. Identifying himself, he told them a young man dressed in black slacks and a pink shirt, approximately five foot four inches tall, shaved head and slender, would be exiting the school in the next few minutes. The police were prepared to follow the suspected drug dealer or to pick him up if necessary.

Ending the call, Ben approached Rex and said, "I'd like to talk to you."

"What do you want, kid?"

"My name is Ben. I'm with the Detective Company."

"Oh, my. Am I under arrest or something, Benny?" Rex said laughing.

"No, but whatever that guy just sold you, will make you very sick. It won't help you swim any faster tomorrow. It will make you throw up."

"I don't know what you're talking about," Rex said looking around the room.

"May I have the bottle he just gave you?"

"What bottle? He gave me nothin'!"

"I don't blame you for lying about this, but listen to me. One of your teammates has gotten sick each meet for the past several weeks because of taking a drug. Now you've got the same stuff that made your teammates sick. If you take it, you'll get sick and hurt your team's chances of winning tomorrow's meet, let alone the state meet in a couple of weeks."

"I tell you I don't know what you're talking about."

"How about giving me that bottle, Rex," Ben said keeping his voice low despite his excitement. "You have the talent right now to win your event but that drug will make you sick. Trust me and give it to me. You will be helping the police catch this guy!"

Rex reached into his pocket and pulled out a small bottle. He gave it to Ben. "I don't know why I'm doing this but I trust you, Benny. Please try to keep my name out of this."

"I will do my best, Rex, but the important thing is to stop this guy!"

Ben called Maggie on the phone. She met him

outside the front door of the school. They drove to
the forensic laboratory of the state police so the
substance could be analyzed.

They then drove to the Centerville Police
Station and were told that due to Ben's quick
thinking, the suspect had been identified. The
police had followed the suspect from the high
school to a house east of town. Officer Brink and
his partner were in a patrol car keeping the house
under surveillance and would like Maggie and Ben
to join them.

The two sleuths drove to the house. After a
quick review of the situation, Ben and Officer
Brink went up to the door and knocked. Maggie
parked next to the police car and watched Ben as
he worked on his first case. The same man who
had talked to Rex came to the door.

Ben's heart was thumping in his chest with the
thrill of being so close to solving his first case.
But being in the right, he felt brave and knew he
had the law on his side.

"What do you want?" asked the drug dealer
eyeing Ben and the policeman.

"We want to talk to you about drugging athletes at the high school," said Ben.

"I don't know what you're talking about," the dealer yelled, about to slam the door.

"I've got it on film," Ben said as Officer Brink pushed his foot against the door. "You're dead in the water, so you might as well come clean. You'll be picked out of a lineup by most of the star swimmers on the high school swim team. It would really be best to confess this thing and maybe the judge can be helpful."

"You're crazy!"

"Your call. Cooperate with us and you might get a break. Continue to lie and it will get tougher for you."

Spotting the police car pulling into the driveway, the dealer dashed out the door past Ben and the officer. He jumped over the porch railing and ran toward the back of the house. Ben and Officer Brink followed close behind. "Give yourself up," Ben yelled, breathing hard. "The drug you gave the swimmers is being analyzed right now."

The drug dealer fell and Ben tripped, falling on top of him. "I bet the lab report will show the drug makes a person throw up. The swimmer gets sick and cannot compete. And you probably get lots of money when the opposing team wins."

"Hey, get off of me. I'm not a gambler!"

"I didn't say you were," said Ben as Officer Brink jerked the dealer to his feet and handcuffed him. "You see that the opponents win the swim meets so gamblers collect the money. My guess is they give you a cut of the winnings."

As the police read the dealer his rights, the dealer moaned, "I need a lawyer."

"Yes, you do," said Ben with feeling. " You've been caught by The Detective Company. Like a bug, you're right in the middle of the spider's web with no place to go."

"All right, I did it. But I'm not taking the rap for this by myself. I was just helping some guys get some easy money."

"You tell the lawyer and the judge all about that. We simply need your confession to get justice done."

"I did it, but it wasn't my idea, honest..."

30

"As I said, tell it to the judge," Ben replied, smug with pride. The Detective Company had successfully solved one more crime.

The criminal was brought to trial where the whole story came out. The ring was extensive, touching many high schools throughout the state and it wasn't just swimming. It was basketball, football and plans had been made to enter the baseball and soccer venues. Both girls and boys teams were involved. Jail terms and fines were handed out and it appeared that The Detective Company had spoiled a very lucrative operation.

The substance in the bottle was analyzed and found to be a high dose of an antidote that causes people to throw up. It is prescribed for someone who has taken poison and it helps get the poison out of the body.

The criminals had put a couple of tablespoons of the substance into small bottles and passed it off as something that would help an athlete, when in·

31

fact, it only causes the body to react violently and zap it of its energy.

All of the athletes who took the drug said they did so because they truly thought it was a legal substance. But when they became too sick to compete, they told no one as they did not want to be disciplined for taking something to enhance their performance. They each apologized to their team, coach, principal and parents. Each sent a letter to Maggie and Ben thanking them for solving **The Case of the Absent Swimmer.**

Ben was recognized by the Centerville School Board. He was introduced by the high school principal at a sports assembly and given a standing ovation by all the students. He received a proclamation from the Student Council thanking him for his investigative work and helping the high school swim team capture the state swimming title.

The End

The Case of the Hidden Bones

Unlocking the battered door, a musty smell hit Jack's nostrils and he slowly descended the steps below the auditorium's stage, his footsteps making a hollow echo. The lonely light bulb in the center of the large storage room gave out poor illumination.

Mrs. Tuttle had given Jack instructions to go to the storage room to find a black box containing scripts for the spring skit "I Love Daffodils." Next week was try-outs and everyone interested would need a copy of the script to practice.

There were boxes everywhere on shelves and stacked on the floor. Very few had labels on them to give a clue to their contents. Jack opened a box of silk flowers, doilies and an old phone; obviously play props. Another box was full of scripts for the play "One Fine Summer."

At last he spied a box that was black, high on a shelf in the corner farthest from the door. "I hope that's not it," thought Jack "It will be very heavy if full of books." Pulling a small stepladder over to the shelf, Jack stood on tiptoe on the top of the ladder. Opening the lid, he peered in, gasped and fell off the ladder. Frmp.

Jack's eyes were large as he quickly got up. Running up the steps to the doorway, he exited the storage room and slammed the door. Jack ran out of the empty auditorium and headed down the hall to the rooms of Maggie McMillan where The Detective Company had their meetings. School was over for the day and Jack totally forgot to report in to Mrs. Tuttle about the mission she had sent him on.

Rushing into the complex, Jack spied Hannah sitting by the phone. She was reading the assigned history chapter in Braille. Her dog, Mellow, reacting to Jack's excitement, lifted her head and looked up at Jack. Although Hannah has extremely poor eyesight, she is an excellent student and an outstanding member of The Detective Company. It is her job to man the phones whenever she can after school.

"Hannah," Jack cried in a rush, his breathing labored. "Is Maggie going to be here today?"

"Maggie is out of town until the end of the week working on that murder case in the northern part of the state," replied Hannah. "I thought everyone knew that."

"Oh, I forgot. Listen, Hannah, I just found a dead body under the auditorium stage," Jack whispered, still panting.

"Oh, I must call the police," Hannah said lifting the phone receiver. "Are you sure the person is dead?"

"Dead for sure, " Jack replied. "It's a skeleton. It must have been hidden down in the storage room for a long, long time."

"Maybe it's just a plastic Halloween thing," Hannah suggested. "Could you see it clearly?"

"What's going on?" asked Tom entering the room, followed by Drew.

"Jack just found a skeleton hidden under the stage of the auditorium," answered Hannah.

"A what?" asked Drew while he checked the volume of his hearing aid. He was not sure he had read the lips of Hannah correctly.

"A skeleton! He thinks it was a real person that has been hidden down there for years."

"Aren't you going to call the police?" asked Tom.

"Before I call anyone, we need to investigate this further. It may just be a cardboard or plastic skeleton used for Halloween decoration. Why don't the three of you go back to check it out."

"Oh," said Jack, looking at the key in his hand. "I forgot to tell Mrs. Tuttle that I did not find the box she sent me down there for. Hannah may be right about it being a Halloween prop so let's use Mrs. Tuttle's key to return to the scene and then stop by her room on the way back. But I am glad you two are coming with me as backup. This thing is still giving me the gruesomes."

The three detectives retraced Jack's steps to the auditorium. They walked down the aisle toward the stage, each giving the others courage to investigate Jack's findings.

"I did not even know there was a storage room under the stage," said Drew as Jack once again unlocked the door. Putting the key back into his pocket, the three timidly stepped into the big room still dimly lit by the single bulb.

"That's the box, over there," said Jack pointing.

"Let's pull it down so we can see inside better," suggested Tom.

Jack climbed the ladder once more and pulled the box forward so that Drew and Tom could help lift it down. As he backed down the ladder, the three placed the box on the floor.

"It seems pretty heavy to contain plastic or cardboard," observed Tom. "Okay, let's open it."

Carefully lifting the lid, the three students stood looking in horror at the bones of a skeleton that grinned up at them with hollow eyes. The skeleton was wrapped in heavy transparent plastic and had what appeared to be tan worms falling off of it.

"Let's get out of here," Drew yelled and the three dashed from the room slamming the door behind them.

"I have to see Mrs. Tuttle and return this key," said Jack, obviously shaken. "Come with me."

"Where are we going?" asked Drew not hearing Jack's comment.

"To Mrs. Tuttle's room," answered Jack, still breathing heavily. "This is her key to the stage storage room."

"Are you going to tell her what we found?" asked Drew.

"I don't know. Perhaps we should tell the police first."

The three students rounded the corner of the hall and came to Mrs. Tuttle's door. It was locked and the interior was dark.

"She must have gone home," Jack said. "She told me to slide the key under the door if she was gone and to put the box of scripts on the floor next to the door."

"I think you had better keep the key so the police can get into the room," said Tom.

Once more the detectives headed back to The Detective Company offices.

"Well, was I right? Is it a Halloween decoration?" asked Hannah hearing their footsteps as they entered the room.

"Hannah," said Drew walking over to her side. "It is a real skeleton and its flesh has been eaten by worms and they look like they are dead as well."

"Since this man or woman has been dead for a long time, maybe we should wait for Maggie to help us with this," said Jack. "Rushing to the police will take the case out of our hands and I would like to do some investigating first."

"I don't know," said Hannah. "This is a serious matter. The police should be notified."

"Oh, we will notify them as soon as we complete the investigation," said Jack. "Everyone in town knows we are great at solving crimes. This could really make us famous!"

"That's a good idea," said Drew after there was a quiet pause.

"Okay, we can let it go for a day or two while we ask around about missing people from the school and the area," said Hannah with a reluctant sigh.

"Should we inform the other members of The Detective Company?" asked Tom.

"We have a meeting scheduled for the day after tomorrow. That's Wednesday. We can tell everyone then. In the meantime, we must keep this between the four of us. Agreed?" asked Jack.

"Agreed," everyone said in unison.

"**The Case of the Hidden Bones**," said Jack. "My first real case!"

That night at the supper table, Jack wanted to tell his parents about his new case. However, remembering his agreement with the others, he knew he must keep quiet about it for at least another day or two. Taking a deep breath while holding a spoonful of ice-cream, Jack looked at his parents and suddenly asked, "Are there any missing persons in Centerville that have been missing for a long time?"

"I don't know, Jack," said his mother. "Why are you asking?"

"Oh, I'm just wondering," answered Jack.

"Is this about a school assignment?" queried his father.

"Sort of..." replied Jack.

Jack jumped up and began clearing the table, his job tonight. He and his older brother Dan went to the kitchen to begin loading the dishwasher.

"What happens to a body after it dies?" Jack asked Dan.

"Oooh!" answered Dan. "That's a gross question. It rots, like an old potato."

43

"Does it smell bad, too?"

"Of course. Doesn't the potato smell bad?"

"But what if the potato was wrapped up real good in a plastic bag. Would it still smell?" asked Jack, needing information.

"Probably not, unless the plastic had a hole in it. Why are you asking about such a gross subject?" asked Dan, looking disgusted.

"Oh, I was just wondering," replied Jack, rinsing off a plate and handing it to Dan who put it in the rack of the machine.

"You'd better stop watching those scary movies," countered Dan.

The next day, Jack told Mrs. Tuttle that he had not found the box of scripts in the storage room. "That's okay, Jack," she answered, "I will ask Miss Young if she stored them somewhere else last spring. Do you have my key?"

Reluctantly, Jack returned the key to Mrs. Tuttle.

During the day, the four detectives asked

44

several people if anyone from school had been missing for a long time. They not only asked the teachers but the students as well.

"Has anyone been missing from this area for a long time," Jack asked Janitor Joe.

"Why are you asking that?" replied Joe, looking suspicious.

"I'm thinking about doing a paper on missing persons for a class," answered Jack feeling very uncomfortable under the stare of the man with the big broom.

"I don't think anyone has ever been missing in our little town," said Joe, his eyes narrowing as he looked at Jack.

"Okay, thanks anyway," said Jack as he scurried down to The Detective Company complex.

The three detectives who knew about the mystery, were already in the room when Jack arrived. Ben, Bree, Nick, Katie, Sharon and David were there as well. It was a full quorum of the members so Jack called for a meeting since everyone was present.

Quickly, Jack informed the members of his discovery the day before. Everyone began to talk in whispers as is often done when someone has passed away. All agreed that since time was not of the essence, it would be best to await Maggie's return to get her expert advice on what to do in the case of a murder.

The gravity of the situation was both frightening and exciting to the group. Several members agreed to use the microfilm room of the library the following day during study hall. Perhaps scanning the old newspapers from the past twenty-five years would provide a valuable clue.

Being committed members of The Detective Company, they respected Jack's request that this new case be kept between the ten of them until Maggie's return. They reasoned that the person responsible for the murder might leave town before their investigation was complete if the details of the case were told.

The following day after school, the group met for their regular Wednesday meeting. Each took a turn reporting their investigation. No one had found a case of murder where the body was still missing in the newspaper archives. In fact there was just one questionable death that had made the papers and that was a hit-and-run automobile accident more than fifteen years ago.

More folks had been asked if there was anyone missing. The druggist had told David that his son had been missing for two years but had returned home and was now in college.

"This must be a stranger," said Hannah with a sigh.

"But the murderer could be someone we all know," added Jack. "Yesterday, I talked with the janitor. You know, the tall one named Joe."

Everyone nodded. "Joe has been janitor as long as I can remember," said Katie. "He doesn't talk very much but he seems nice enough."

"Well, he wasn't so nice when I asked him about missing persons," offered Jack. "He seemed to act very suspicious about my questions."

"Oooh, do you think he could be a murderer?" asked Sharon, looking behind her.

"Everyone is a suspect right now," answered Jack, "but don't forget that everyone is not guilty until proven otherwise."

All the members nodded their heads in agreement. Due to the seriousness of the case, everyone was a bit jittery. They again solemnly vowed to keep the mystery a secret until Maggie's return. The Detective Company left the building in pairs or threesomes that evening. Hannah's mother came to pick her up and Katie got a ride with them.

The following morning, all members were in high spirits. They high-fived in the hallways and smiled greetings. Maggie was due in that afternoon and they were eager to share Jack's case with her.

Toward the end of the day, just before last hour, Tom spied Maggie's van in the parking lot. "She's here," he told one of the members and the word quickly spread.

Maggie was surprised when all members of The Detective Company came running to the complex, looking toward Jack to tell Maggie the news. "Everyone take a seat," said Maggie, laughing at their enthusiasm. "We must have a new case brewing. Whose is it?"

"Jack's," said Hannah, leaving her seat at the phone to come forward with her dog Mellow to attend the gathering. Nick quickly pulled a chair over for her.

"Okay, Jack. Spill it." said Maggie with good humor.

"There's been a murder," Jack said looking like the world had come to an end.

"What happened? What are the facts about the case?" asked Maggie.

Everyone began talking at once and Maggie put her hand up. When silence fell, she turned to Jack. "Now, tell me right from the beginning what has happened."

"Mrs. Tuttle sent me down to the storage room under the auditorium stage and I opened a long black box and found a body inside. It has been there a long time as the flesh has been eaten off and it is now a skeleton. We thought about calling the police but decided to wait for you to come back as the body has been there a long time."

"Well, you should have called the police. Death is a matter of greatest urgency even if the death appears to have happened long ago," said Maggie. "Hannah, call the police station and get Detective Burgoon on the line for me."

Hannah returned to her seat at the phone and placed the call. Maggie took the phone when Detective Burgoon came on the line. "Good afternoon," Maggie began, "I have an urgent matter here at the school and we require police assistance immediately."

Maggie sat quietly listening and the members of The Detective Company exchanged anxious looks. Then Maggie told him, "It seems the members of the Detective Company have discovered a body under the stage in our auditorium. Can you come right away?"

There was a short pause and Maggie said, "Thank you."

Maggie hung up the phone and asked, "Who was in the storage room and saw the body?" When Jack and Tom raised their hands, Bree nudged Drew and faced him to say, "Raise your hand, Drew."

Drew looked at Maggie who asked, "Drew, were you with Jack and Tom when the body was found?" When Drew nodded his head, Maggie said, "The three of you come with me. You need to talk to the police when they get here."

51

Maggie and the detectives walked down the hall to the office. As the secretary handed Maggie a key to the storage room off the auditorium, sirens could be heard coming toward the school.

The foursome met the policemen in the hallway and after a quick introduction, the group moved forward through the doors of the auditorium. Jack spied Janitor Joe looking at them and then he appeared to hurry away.

Marching down the aisle toward the stage, the student detectives felt important and ready to show the evidence to the police.

Maggie unlocked the door and turned on the light at the wall switch. The three students gasped as the box was no longer on the floor.

"It's gone," wailed Drew.

"No, it isn't," said Jack as he saw that it had been replaced on the shelf. Pointing it out to the officers, he waited to see if the box was now empty. If it was, their mistake of not notifying the police was a grave one.

But when the officers took the box down and opened it, there was the skeleton still looking a bit jovial despite the seriousness of the situation. The

52

officers told the students to stand back while they carefully inspected the skeleton.

"The skull has a large metal hook coming out of the top," observed Detective Burgoon.

"Ooh," said Jack. "That must be how they killed him!"

The officers pulled the skeleton out of the bag and began to laugh. The students looked horrified that something so terrible could be humorous. The officers then showed the students that the skeleton's bones were held to each other with metal links.

"Aha!" said Maggie. "This is a skeleton that is used in a medical laboratory or something."

"But wait," said Jack. "Look at all those dried up worms in the bag. How did all that get in there?"

"It's just old excelsior," answered the other officer. "It's packing material. They used this stuff before bubble-wrap and Styrofoam peanuts were developed."

The next day, the Centerville newspaper carried the story entitled **The Case of the Hidden Bones**. The State University Science Department had reported thirty years ago that their skeleton had been stolen but it had never been recovered. It was believed at the time that some college group had pulled a prank but it had long been forgotten. How it got to be stored in the Centerville Middle School storage room under the auditorium was a mystery.

Jack was quoted in the paper how he had thought he had discovered a murder; but he was glad he had just found a missing skeleton for the University and not a victim of foul play.

One day soon afterward, Jack asked Janitor Joe if he had attended State University but Joe just shook his head and kept mopping the classroom where Jack had located him to ask that question.

It was a fun story to tell and retell. A story that had a delightful ending and was another solved case for The Detective Company.

The End

The Case of the
Disappearing
Medals

The Case of the Disappearing Medals

"Look out, Maggie," Katie cried at the same moment that Maggie quickly pushed hard on the brake with her right hand. A brown pickup truck glided across the path of Maggie's special accessibility van, missing the bumper by inches.

"That man ran a red light," Katie exclaimed.

"Yes, he did," Maggie agreed. "Thank goodness we were able to slow down in time for him to miss us. A driver not only needs to drive with care, but must watch out for what other drivers are doing."

"That scared me for a second," admitted Katie.

"I like the fact that you are so alert, Katie. Despite the fact that you were giving me details of your new miniature icebox, you were also aware of what was happening around you. Your watchfulness should help you solve our mystery today."

"I am excited about visiting the Special Olympics office with you," Katie said, smiling. "When you talked to Ms. Adams on the phone, did she give you any clues as to what has happened to the medals? The children will be so disappointed if there are no medals awarded after the competition."

"She has no idea of why the medals have disappeared," Maggie said in reply. "Here we are now."

Maggie's van rode beneath a huge banner announcing "SPECIAL OLYMPIC GAMES -- STATE COMPETITION." The campus was alive with excited people attending the annual event.

The parking lot was full of cars. School buses were parked together like soldiers at attention. Near the door to the office, a space reserved for handicap accessibility was available and the van glided to a stop. As the van door rolled open, the sound of the cheering crowd met their ears. Katie was lowered to the ground where she wheeled her chair onto the pavement. Maggie pushed a button to gain access to the platform, and soon she was on the ground to join Katie. The equipment retreated into the van and the door rolled shut.

As the two wheeled toward the entrance of the office, the cheering stopped and they could hear someone calling, "Maggie, Katie." Stopping to look toward the stadium, they spied Sharon running toward them.

"Hi!" Sharon said, breathing hard from running. "Are you here to watch the games? I am in the fifty-yard dash next. My coach told me to

61

come right back as soon as I told you 'hi'."

"You look great, Sharon," said Katie, reaching out to squeeze her hand. "Maggie and I are here to work on a mystery."

"A mystery? Here at the Olympics?" asked Sharon, her eyes growing big. "Did they ask The Detective Company to solve it?"

"Yes, but it has nothing to do with you athletes," Maggie said reassuringly. "We are so proud you are competing. We know you will do your best for Centerville."

"I will try to win. But Coach says it is okay to lose. It is only important to do our best," Sharon told them. "I'd better go back now." Smiling and waving, she ran back to her teammates.

As Maggie and Katie approached the office, they read the oath over the front door: *Let me win, but if I cannot win, let me be brave in the attempt.* The mission statement on a plaque to the right of the door read, *To provide year-round sports training and athletic competition in a variety of Olympic-type sports for children and adults with mental retardation.*

"Do I look okay, Maggie?" Katie asked, smoothing her dress.

"You look like a good detective ready to go to work," Maggie replied.

Leslie Adams, the Executive Director, welcomed them inside and asked them to follow her. "Since this is your first trip to our office, let me give you a quick tour." Leslie was brief in pointing out things as she wanted to get Katie and Maggie working on the case.

"As we approach the storeroom, you will notice the sports photos on either side of the wall. We're proud to serve 30,000 athletes in 32 sports." Leslie opened a couple of big doors and before them was a huge room used to store materials needed to host the Games. One side held basketballs, hockey sticks, skis, bobsleds and other winter game equipment. On the other side were empty cages that obviously were used to store summer game supplies. "This is our storeroom. You'll find everything that we use in our games in this huge area."

"Great storage space, Leslie," commented Maggie. "And it is so neatly organized."

"Yes. Oh, please overlook that pile of metal. We've been replacing our heating ducts. The University maintenance department will be carting this away. In fact, they should have been here this morning. They're usually so prompt, but with the games and three thousand athletes on campus, they probably have their hands full with all kinds of trash removal and helping us put on a smooth operation here.

"Our business center with staff offices is here across the hall. But we're running out of time. Let me take you to the room where the medals were last seen." Leslie led Katie and Maggie into the conference room called the "Nerve Center" for the games. There were boxes all around and although appearing to be organized, one would have to be aware of the setup to find anything.

"Would you care for some coffee or something?" Leslie asked.

"Katie and I are a lot alike, but we have different desires when it comes to refreshments. Katie is a diet cola fan and I am a decaf coffee drinker. No cream, thank you."

"I can please both of you. Be back in a moment."

Katie looked at Maggie. "What do you think all the little boxes are for?"

"They are filled with cards. Probably registration forms of the participants."

"The big ones on the floor are mostly empty," observed Katie. "Just this one over here that has a few T-shirts in it. The shirts have the Special Olympics logo on them. I guess we can assume that all those boxes once were full of shirts. The shirt that Sharon was wearing looked like these."

"Good thinking, Katie!"

Leslie returned with the coffee and a cold diet cola. "Thanks for coming here to help us. We don't have much time to solve this very frustrating dilemma. Our medals are gone, hundreds of them. We've nothing to give our athletes for all their hard work and earned victories. They have been training for months in swimming, weightlifting, track and field, boccie ball and volleyball, to name just a few, but with the hope of winning a medal."

"We can understand your frustration, Leslie and we will begin our investigation right away. Is this the room where the medals were last seen?" Maggie asked.

"Yes. They were delivered in a big box and placed in this conference room unopened. We planned to separate them into various events and have prepared envelopes to keep them organized."

"When you say 'we,' Ms. Adams, who helped you with the medals?" asked Katie.

"Two of our staff, Tracy and Judy, opened the box early this morning and had piled all of the medals on this long table. They planned to sort them with one each of gold, silver and bronze to place in the prepared envelopes, with extras set aside for any ties."

"I think our first task is to talk to Tracy and Judy, as they must have been the last to handle the medals," Katie said, thinking how best to proceed to solve the mystery.

"I have talked to each of them and they have no clue as to where they could have gone."

"I'm sure they have told you all they know, but we'd like to talk to them as well," Maggie explained.

"Not a problem. I figured you would."

"Oh, before we talk to them, we'll want to know who has access to this area where the medals were last seen," Katie added.

"Well, I do, and of course, Tracy and Judy do. Actually it is not a secured area. Anybody can come in here. It's just a room we use for meetings next to the storage area."

"Has anyone given you or any member of your staff a threatening call or mail or message of any kind?" Katie asked.

"Not that I know of. I can't understand why anyone would want a couple of thousand medals. They are not valuable and don't mean anything to anyone except the athletes."

"If they were made of real gold, silver and bronze, they'd have plenty of value," murmured Katie with a frown. "Let us do a little brain-storming for a few minutes."

"Let me know when you want to talk to Tracy and Judy," Leslie said, going to the door. "We all want this mystery solved and soon."

Katie is thirteen years old, a bright and talented middle school student. She bonded with

Maggie almost as soon as they met at The Detective Company. They are a carbon copy of each other with about thirty years separating them. They are both neat people, very smart, both wheelchair users, and both love to help others.

Maggie is a marvelous model for Katie in so many ways. She helped Katie accept her disability. She taught her investigative skills which also paid off in the classroom. Most of going to school is about solving problems, thinking things through and drawing conclusions from what we read, see or hear.

The two also share a hobby and that is unusual. By accident one day they discovered that each of them collects miniatures for their doll houses. Actually Maggie has been collecting the miniatures since her youth. Needless to say, they are friends and they will undoubtedly demonstrate this day why they make a good detective team.

"This simply has to be a case of misplacing these things, Maggie," Katie said, scratching her head and then carefully patting her hair into place. "I cannot believe some thief would come in here and take all those medals. Nobody in his right mind would want to disappoint our Special Olympians."

"That's the phrase that gives us plenty of business, Katie. 'In his right mind...' The people that have no compassion for others are the ones who are disruptive and bring upsetting circumstances to a lot of folks."

"Well, we only have a couple of hours to bring this to a close. What should we do, Maggie?"

"Well, this is your case, Katie. We have no time for you to ask other members of The Detective Company for their ideas, so I guess you need to figure out how best to solve this case."

"Right now, I can't think of a thing."

"Remember what you have learned in our meetings about working back from the crime and thinking of possible events or activities that may have occurred."

"I know, Maggie, but when I do that, all I can conclude is that anyone in the world could

69

come in here and take them for any reason."

"Yes, but most likely only one person took them. Think it out, Katie," Maggie encouraged.

Katie took out her notepad and wrote down the facts.

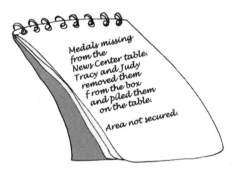

Medals missing from the News Center table. Tracy and Judy removed them from the box and piled them on the table.

Area not secured.

On the next page, she made a list but had nothing to fill in the blanks.

Motive:

Suspect:

Time of Theft:

Witnesses:

Evidence at the Scene:

"I suppose one theory could be that someone in the Special Olympics is sabotaging the games, someone who would want to get Leslie into trouble and maybe fired," Katie thought out loud.

"That's a good theory, Katie. Now you're cooking."

"But isn't that unlikely?" Katie asked.

"Probably," Maggie answered. "But detectives have to look at every angle and after all, we don't know all the people here or the reasons they might be unhappy. The board of these prestigious games will be very unhappy if this situation is not resolved and they will probably hold the director responsible."

"The athletes will be disappointed, but think of all the people that will be upset: the parents, the coaches, the chaperones, why even the bus drivers," Katie added. "And every hometown newspaper will be taking photos of their athletes and will expect bright medals around their necks."

"Good thinking, Katie. We should talk to the person who has their finger on the pulse of interoffice personnel and knows about potential conflicts."

"You two sleuths ready to talk to Tracy and Judy?" Leslie asked, as she walked into the room.

"Would either of them have an insight into

the personalities of all the office staff? You know, who knows gossip. Who knows what really goes on here?" asked Maggie.

"Well, I'd like to think that would be me, but I'm probably not the best person to talk to. I guess you need to talk to Carrie, our receptionist. Do you want to talk to her?"

"Yes, please," Katie said.

"I'll ask her to come in."

In a few moments, Carrie arrived and said, "How can I help you?"

"We're wondering if there is anyone on the staff who might have taken the medals to cause trouble," Katie said.

"Oh, no. I can assure you that nobody would do that. We all love the athletes and would do absolutely nothing to interfere with their having a good time."

"That's good," Katie said and then sat quietly looking at Carrie, waiting to see if she had anything else to add.

"And for the record, Leslie is admired and respected. No one would intentionally bring any problem to bear on Leslie or anyone who works here for that matter."

"Okay. Thanks for talking with us, Carrie. We wanted to check out the conspiracy and sabotage theory," Maggie said.

"Glad I could help." Carrie left after expressing her hope that Katie and Maggie could solve the case of the disappearing medals.

"Well, I guess I hit a brick wall on that theory," Katie said with a sigh as she looked down at her empty list.

"That's true, Katie, but at least you can rule out that theory and concentrate on another theory."

"My second thought was the medals could have been taken by athletes," Katie said, happy to have a quick backup theory. "You know, like a kid in the candy store. Once someone sees what is here, the prize, you might say; an athlete might have simply been spellbound with seeing so many medals and put them all in a box and walked away with them."

"That makes sense," Maggie replied. "The

box would be very heavy and also the athlete or athletes would have to put them someplace where a chaperone, coach, parent or bus driver would not see them and report the misbehavior."

"I'm going to take a spin outside and look around," Katie said. "Maybe they hid the box in a grove of trees, or put it behind the bushes with the plan to pick it up later."

Katie drove her power chair to the front door, pushed the automatic door opener and sped through the doorway, her curls bouncing as she put on her best sleuth guise. Katie spent ten minutes looking in a host of logical places where a thief might have tossed or hidden the medals. She searched around the Special Olympics office building and actually rode out from the building about one hundred yards in all directions but didn't spy any suspicious box. Frustrated, she drove back to the office building.

"Find anything, Katie?" Maggie asked.

"No. Nothing turned up."

"Well, once again, you can check that theory off of your list. Not learning anything is just as much solving a crime as having the solution appear

74

before your eyes. The good investigator needs to rule out the hunches and this usually happens before hitting upon the real motive."

"Since I inspected the outside, I've also got to go on a search of the inside of the building." Katie powered her chair again and set off to look into each nook and cranny of the building. She had no idea that so much "stuff" needed to be stored in order to put on a wide variety of sports competitions. But for all her effort, she didn't find the box of disappearing medals.

She was about to leave the storage room and head back to the conference room to talk to Maggie when she stopped to steer clear of a piece of metal that had obviously fallen from the pile that was scheduled for maintenance department pickup. She backed up and turned her wheels so she would miss the metal piece. A sharp piece of metal could damage her wheel.

When Katie rode into the conference room, she told Maggie, "No luck. Let's talk to Tracy and Judy." Leslie was paged and asked to have Tracy and Judy come to the conference room for an interview. The two women appeared within seconds.

"Hi, this is Katie, the lead detective on this case and I'm Maggie McMillan. I assume one of you is Judy and the other, Tracy."

"Yes, I'm Tracy and this is Judy." The four shook hands and gathered around the conference table.

"We understand that you two were the last to see the medals in the office. Is that true?" Katie asked.

"I guess so. We had taken all of them out of the huge box and piled them up on the table. It was time for our coffee break and we left. When we returned about fifteen minutes later, they were gone and so was the box!"

"Did anyone see anyone else in the area or even in the parking lot or anyone strange for that matter?"

"No, I don't recall anyone," Tracy said, while Judy shook her head indicating she had seen no strangers either. "Everyone I saw had a legitimate reason to be around."

"Okay then, who did you see?" Katie asked.

"Well, let's see. I saw Leslie, and Fran was in the coffee break room. The receptionist was at the front desk. Out the window, I saw Hilda in the parking lot coming in from checking out the venues. I also saw a State University maintenance employee getting into his truck out front. He must have been picking up some litter. We get a large volume of litter during the Games. I didn't see anyone else."

"Thanks. Nobody you saw was a stranger or someone who didn't belong where you saw them, right?" Katie asked.

"That's right."

"Wow," said Katie with a sigh. "This is a strange case, don't you think?"

"It's like the medals simply evaporated from the table. Very strange," Judy said, shaking her head.

As Tracy and Judy left, Katie told Maggie she was going to the restroom. She wheeled out of the conference room and headed down the hall. She glanced at the floor near the entrance to the men's room and what she saw made her stop. There was a distinct print of a large boot. The floor from the entrance throughout the front room was dirty from tracked-in mud following the light morning rain. The mud was obliterated even more by the wheel marks of Katie's and Maggie's chairs. But the print in front of the men's room door was distinct and unmarred. Katie drew no conclusion from the print but mentioned it to Maggie when she returned to the conference room.

Maggie suggested that Leslie be called back in. When she entered the room, she listened to Katie. "It seems that all of the names I've heard since we arrived and all the people we've seen are women. Right?"

"I guess so. We have several men on staff but they arrived early this morning and went straight out to set up tents over registration areas and scoring tables. They were also putting up chalk lines in some of the venue areas. Now they are still out there bringing drinking water to the sites and guiding athletes to their events. I guess you are right. Only women have been in the office today."

"Has any man been here today?" asked Katie, her eyes wide with interest.

"Well, I guess not, now that you mention it. As I said, the men on our staff were all assigned to sports competition areas and had no reason to come into the main office today."

Katie suggested that Leslie go with them to the entrance to the men's restroom. They did and the three women looked at the clear boot print. "Hmmm. It looks like a boot that a construction worker would wear."

"Yeah, I was thinking the same thing," Katie said. "How about the workers that replaced the heating ducts. Could one of them be wearing a boot that would leave a print like that?"

"I guess so, but they finished working here two days ago and the cleaning crew mop and vacuum every evening. This boot print is fresh."

"So you conclude that a man came through this door since the building was opened this morning?"

"Yes, definitely," Leslie said.

"Maybe the medals are in the bathroom," Katie said hopefully.

"Let's go in and look around." Leslie knocked on the door to make sure nobody would be

embarrassed by the intrusion of three women.
Silence. Leslie walked in. Maggie and Katie
followed. Each was careful not to step or wheel on
the fresh prints that continued into the room.
Inside they found no box of medals but looking
into the trash barrel, they did find a couple of paper
towels that were used to dry hands. Maggie
suggested they leave the towels undisturbed as they
may be evidence.

Back in the conference room, Maggie and
Katie continued to discuss the case and try to
determine their next steps. Before Leslie left the
room, she looked at her watch and said, "The first
medals are to be awarded in forty-five minutes. Is
there any chance that the first athlete will have a
shiny medal hanging from his or her neck?"

Katie looked at
Maggie, took a deep
breath and looked up
at Leslie. "I'd like to be
more reassuring, but as
of this second I don't
have a clue as to who
took the medals or
where they might be."

80

"I'll get the word to all of the event coordinators that the medals may not arrive and to be prepared to explain to everyone that they have been misplaced and will be awarded as soon as they are found," Leslie said, looking disappointed.

"I have a great deal of faith in Katie and I'm sure she will solve it in time," Maggie said with a smile.

Leslie smiled and left. Katie turned to Maggie and said, "Thanks for the vote of confidence but I think we are back to zero."

"Simply put all the evidence together, Katie. Solving a case is like putting a puzzle together. You simply need to make sure the pieces of information are connecting and sooner or later a picture will begin to form. That's what you need to do now."

"But nothing seems to be coming together."

"I'll tell you what, Katie. I think I've solved the case. I'm not going to tell you what is on my mind, but we think so much alike. I think that you simply haven't organized the information we've gotten this morning. Once the information fits, you'll have it solved."

81

"Well, I'd sure like to make sense of it."

"You will, but if you don't solve it in the next few minutes, I'll not embarrass us by with-holding the solution to a mystery. I'll tell you my theory, and if I'm right, medals will soon hang from the necks of our victorious athletes."

"You've got it solved, Maggie?"

"I think so and all I did was put the information together. Give it your best thinking, Katie, and it should fall into a logical pattern. I think we should simply be quiet for a minute so you can run the information through your mind. Silence is often a good friend of the detective."

Katie did what her mentor suggested. She took a deep breath and lowered her head. As she twisted a curl around her finger, she tried to think of everything she had seen and heard so far to see if any patterns would become logical. After a couple of minutes, she moved her attention to the notepad where she'd written information obtained from interviews and some observations she'd made.

Maggie remained silent to let Katie think and reason. After a few minutes, Maggie said, "Okay, now I'm going to teach you another trick of successful detectives."

"Good, because this isn't helping. I can't see a pattern, Maggie."

"When you're stuck like this, you merely begin to talk it out. Talk like you are explaining what you know to someone sitting next to you. You can talk to me, but if you were alone it would still help to talk out loud as though there was someone there to listen. Often what happens is you hit upon the pattern by listening to yourself. Give it a try."

"Okay, but I'd feel a little silly talking to nobody."

"Then you can tell me, a real person and see if that helps."

"Okay, here goes, Maggie. If this doesn't work, you'll need to solve it because I'll probably be stumped."

"If you don't get it, I'll let you know what I think happened."

Katie looked at her notes, organized some thoughts, and began to talk. "Medals are missing from the conference room of the Special Olympics office. Tracy and Judy took them from the box and put them into a huge pile. They took a coffee break

83

and planned to sort the medals and put them into envelopes when they returned. When they came back, the medals were gone. I've searched outside and inside but I did not find them. A man's fresh boot print was found at the entrance to the men's room in the Special Olympics office. All the people that were seen in the building or the vicinity of the building were women, and...whoops, that's not true... One of the people was a maintenance man getting into his truck."

"Bingo!" Maggie said. "Keep it coming, Katie."

"And the State University maintenance department was to come here to pick up a pile of metal in the storeroom, but strangely they haven't taken it away yet."

"Keep it coming, Katie, you're almost there," Maggie cheered.

"And the man was confused. He thought he was supposed to pick up a pile of <u>medals</u> from the Special Olympics office instead of a pile of <u>metal</u>. So the medals must be in a box at the maintenance department or they are still in the back of the man's truck."

84

"GREAT work, Katie! Good for you. Call Leslie in and give her your solution to the case of the missing medals."

Leslie walked in and Katie said, "We've got it solved."

Maggie interrupted, "No, Katie has it solved. She figured it out. Tell Leslie where her medals are, Katie."

"We think they were picked up by the man from the maintenance department. You were

surprised that he was late picking up the pile of metal. That's because he thought he was to pick up a pile of medals which is what he found here in the conference room. While he was here, he used the restroom. So, if you call the maintenance department, you should find the box of medals."

"Thank you so much, Katie! You are a terrific detective!" Leslie looked at her watch and dashed out of the room to get to a phone.

Leslie called and sure enough, there had been a misunderstanding of the work request. The box of medals was immediately returned to the Special Olympics office. Tracy and Judy quickly organized the medals so that the first set of awards could be presented on time. Leslie drove the office golf cart to the competition managers and with literally only seconds to spare, the medals were placed around the necks of the happy winners.

Parents, fans, coaches, volunteers, chaperones, and the media had no idea of the drama that had taken place behind the scenes to assure that the medals would be there in time to honor the athletes.

Leslie returned to the office with a big "Thank You" for Katie and Maggie. She was relieved to have the case solved. She assured Maggie that The Detective Company would be recognized for their successful investigation of the missing medals. Katie had saved the day, no question about it.

Maggie and Katie got into Maggie's van. As Katie moved her chair into the special spot to lock down her wheels, Maggie turned to look at her.

"Feel good, Katie?"

"Yes, I sure do," Katie replied, clicking her seat belt on. "It was close, but we solved it."

"YOU solved **The Case of the Disappearing Medals**, Katie. You put all of your skills to work and solved the case. Your observations were excellent, your analysis of the evidence was perfect and your thinking was right on the money. And you were right, it didn't make sense to have the medals stolen. It was simply a misunderstanding, but you made sense of it in time for a lot of people to be happy. Good job, I'm proud to have you in The Detective Company."

The End

The Case of the

Missing
Teen

The Case of the Missing Teen

"Go to your room, Will!"

"Ah, Mom."

"NOW!" Mrs. Parker said sternly.

Will got up from his seat at the table and looked at his stepfather. He, in turn, was looking at Will's mother, a sad look in his eyes. Will knew his own dad would have spoken up for his son.

Wistfully eyeing the fresh pan of brownies on the countertop, Will left the kitchen and walked to his bedroom. Looking back, he could see his mother and stepfather clearing the table. Will slammed the door and sitting on his bed, reached for his TV remote control.

Will turned on his favorite channel, but did not pay attention to the dogs that were running around stakes and up ramps. He was angry. Why did his mother get so mad at him all the time? He hadn't said anything bad at the table. He just told her that he wished she would find someone else to yell at once in a while. When his own father had lived with them, dinner was fun. His dad could joke about anything.

Will could hear his mother and stepfather talking but the words were too muffled to hear what they were talking about. He didn't care anyway. He imagined his mother and stepfather probably wished he had never been born. Will used the remote to surf the channels. Stopping to watch a funny advertisement, he went back to his favorite channel.

Now he could hear his mother putting dishes in the dishwasher. His favorite show about crocodiles was starting. Pushing his book bag off the bed, he spread out to enjoy the show. The excitement of the program helped him forget the altercation with his mother.

Toward the end of the program, Will saw his stepfather's ball cap pass his window. Getting up, he watched his mother and stepfather walking arm-in-arm down the driveway. They turned at the sidewalk and headed down the street.

Using the phone extension in his room, Will tried to call his best friend but the line was busy. He just had to talk to someone. Will opened his window and hiked himself up to the sill. Looking back at the TV, he watched as the credits of the program scrolled on the screen. The volume of the TV should give his mother the impression that he was still in his room. Dropping to the ground, he ran through backyards to his best friend's house.

Will knocked on the side door and Mrs. Mason opened it almost immediately.

"Is David home?"

"David," Mrs. Mason called. "Will is here."

David came to the door and said, "Come on in ,Will. I'm doing my geography homework. Did you get your map drawn?"

"No," Will replied. "I was going to do it later. Hey, could we do them together?"

"Mom, is it okay if Will and I do our homework together?" David asked.

"All right, David," Mrs. Mason answered. "But I'd better not hear you two playing games on your computer."

"Thanks, Mom," David said as he led Will to his bedroom.

"I wish I had a computer in my room," Will said.

"You've got a TV and a phone, man. I don't have that!"

"I got sent to my room for mouthing off to my mom," Will confessed after David had closed the door. "I climbed out my window to come over."

"Man, you're going to get into more trouble for sneaking out."

"No, I won't. I left the TV on. She will think I'm in my room. I can climb back in and go to bed. And no one will ever know I was gone."

"Well, let's get to work on our maps. Here, I have extra paper."

The two boys sprawled on the floor and carefully drew a map of the state. They drew a star

for Capital City and a small circle for Centerville. David added the city where he had been born and drew in Round Lake where their summer cabin was located. He used a blue pencil to color the lake. While they worked, Will talked about his situation at home.

"I bet my stepfather wishes I didn't live with them."

"Did he tell you that?" David asked.

"Of course not, but when my mom yells at me, you can tell he doesn't like it. I wish I lived with my dad."

95

"Hey, I have to go all summer when you are at your dad's house. Don't start wishing that you will disappear from my life all together."

"I'm sorry, David. I just get so tired of living where I know no one wants me."

"You could be wrong about this," David said thoughtfully.

"Yeah, maybe. Thanks for letting me make my map with you."

"David," Mrs. Mason called as she knocked on the door. "Will's mother just called and asked that Will come home now."

"Oh, no," Will gasped, his eyes getting large.

"You'd better get going," David said as they scrambled to their feet.

"I'm gone."

Will ran for his house but as he entered his back yard, he slowed down to a walk. He dreaded going into the house.

When he opened the door, he found his mother waiting for him in the kitchen. "All right, young man. You are grounded for one week. No TV, no leaving the house except to go to school. Now go to your room."

Will walked to his room. The door to his bedroom was open. The window had been closed and Will noticed that his TV was no longer in the room. With anger, he slammed the door.

He got ready for bed quickly. While he was in the bathroom, he purposely did not brush his teeth or wash his face.

Will was too upset to fall asleep. When his clock shined the hour of eleven, he heard his mother coming down the hall. Will closed his eyes to pretend sleep. His mother opened the door and softly spoke, "Good night Will. We love you."

But Will did not answer.

Will was still awake when he watched the clock numbers roll over to 2:00 a.m. He had come up with a plan. He quietly got up and opened a book his dad had given him, Mark Twain's *Tom*

Sawyer. He rifled through the book and a tiny key fell out of the pages. Carefully opening his closet door, he took his strong box down from the shelf without making a sound.

Taking the box to his bed, he unlocked it and in the moonlight counted the money inside. It came to $164.52, more than half in coins. Will cut lawns in the summer at his dad's house and both his father and stepfather often gave him some spending money as well. Will had saved every penny he could lay his hands on for over a year. He occasionally skipped lunch at school so he could save the lunch money his mother gave him. David and his other friends would share their lunches with him as they knew he was saving for a computer.

Now, Will pulled on his T-shirt and jeans and pocketed all the money. He raised the window to once again climb out but heard his stepfather coming down the hall.

Will quickly moved off the window sill and bumped his nose on the window jamb. Covering his mouth to avoid yelling out, he stood quietly to listen. He heard his stepfather turn on the light in the bathroom and close the door.

Never moving until he heard the footsteps returning to the master bedroom, Will now felt something warm on his face. Turning on the light, he saw that he had developed a nose bleed. He held his face in his pillow for a few minutes until the bleeding had stopped. Turning off the light, he sat and gave his mission more thought.

If he was missing in the morning, he would probably be caught. It would be better to wait until later. Will pulled his book bag up on the bed and unpacked his notebook, an old sweatshirt, several wrinkled homework papers, some dirty gym socks, and a candy bar wrapper. Silently opening the bottom drawer of his dresser, he took out all the sweatshirts stored there. He placed his notebook in the drawer and covered it with the sweatshirts. He threw the dirty sweatshirt and socks on the closet floor and tossed the papers into his strong box. He locked it and placed the box back on the shelf. He then put the key back in the book and returned it to the bookcase.

Will packed a pair of jeans and three shirts in his book bag. It looked just like it did when it had his books in it. Getting back into bed with his clothes on, he turned the stained pillow over, pulled up the sheet and fell asleep.

"Wake up, Will," his mother called shaking his shoulder. Groggily, he pushed back the sheet to stand.

"William Luke Gooding Parker! What are you doing sleeping in your clothes?"

"My name is not Parker, Mom. My last name is Gooding, just like my dad's!"

"I said, what are you doing sleeping in your clothes?"

"I was tired but hey, now I am ready for school."

"What is that on your face? It looks like dried blood. Uh-oh, did you get up in the night and eat some of my brownies? You change those clothes right now and wash your face!"

Rubbing his head, Will pulled off his jeans and T-shirt and got fresh clothing from the closet. He went into the bathroom to wash his face and comb his hair. As he walked toward the kitchen, he could hear his mother starting the washing machine. Startled, he ran back to his bedroom. With a sigh of relief, he reached into his soiled jeans pocket. Turning his back to the door, he pocketed all his money.

His mother did not speak to him as he ate his cereal. She poured a cup of coffee for herself and then sat down at the table.

"Will, you know that I love you."

"Yeah, Mom."

"You have a nice day," she called as he came from his bedroom carrying his book bag.

"You too, Mom," he said wistfully as she stood, handed him his lunch money and kissed him on the cheek.

He ran out the side door and headed through the back yard to David's house. David came out the door just as Will reached it.

"Hi, Will," David said. "I'm glad to see you lived through the night."

"You forgot to comb your hair again." Will said.

"Oh yeah. You got a comb?"

Will stopped and opened the side pocket of his book bag. As he handed David his comb, he said, "Here you go."

"Man, you even have a comb in there. You got a girlfriend?"

Will gave a snort of disbelief at his friend's comment as they entered the wooded lot that was their shortcut to the school.

"You are my best friend, Dave. I will never forget you."

"Hey, you sound like gloom and doom. Ease up, man! What did your mother and stepfather say when you got home last night?"

"My mom grounded me for a week!"

"Ah, Will, that means you won't be able to goof off with me this Saturday!"

"Sorry."

"What's the matter with you? Did you tell your mom that we were doing homework?" David asked as they came out of the woods.

"She didn't even give me a chance. Hey, I

102

forgot my map. I'd better run back and get it. See you at school."

With a wave, Will ran back into the trees and then stopped. He looked back. David had joined up with a group of boys and they were talking and laughing as they reached the school grounds. Will leaned against a tree and waited until he heard the school bell ring.

Tossing his book bag over his shoulder, Will came out of the woods again but turned toward town instead of toward home or school. He went into the drugstore next to the bus station and bought a magazine. "Aren't you supposed to be in school, son?" asked the man at the counter.

"I'm going on a field trip this morning," Will answered. "I need something to read while I ride."

103

"Well, have a good trip!"

"Thanks," Will said.

Outside, he turned the corner and entered the bus station. The terminal was crowded with people ready to take the next bus out.

"I need a ticket to Capital City," Will told the man at the ticket counter.

"That'll be two dollars even," the man said punching his machine that printed tickets. Will handed the man his lunch money.

The bus arrived in a few minutes and Will climbed on board with the others. Will looked back to see if anyone had observed him getting on the bus. He saw no one he knew and took a seat beside a young woman with a toddler on her lap. The bus rolled out of the station and Will settled back in his seat, his heart hammering with excitement at his success so far.

In the meantime, David kept looking out the classroom window during first hour, but there was no sign of his friend. David hoped that Will did not get into an argument with his mother about the possibility of being late for school.

The trip to the city only took forty minutes and Will got off the bus and headed into the big station. He took two of his precious quarters from his jeans pocket and bought a roll of candy from a machine.

Trying to appear calm, Will got into line to buy a ticket to Dallas. His father lived in a suburb of Dallas and he hoped he would be welcome there even though he was two months early for his summer stay.

"What'll it be, young man?" asked the ticket agent.

"I need a one-way ticket to Dallas."

"You with that lady that just bought a ticket to Dallas a bit ago?"

"What?" Will asked.

"That lady, there," the man said, pointing to a large woman seated nearby. "You'd better be with someone, son. I can't sell a ticket to a youngster."

105

"Oh, her. Yeah, she's my mom. She forgot to buy me a ticket."

"Well, I thought she had too much luggage for one person," the man commented as he rang up the sale. "That will be $122.40. I hope you have the right change. I don't have any one dollar bills."

"Oh, excuse me. I will be right back." Will left the counter. He looked back at the man and saw that he was watching him.

Will walked over to the heavy set woman and said, "Hello."

She smiled at him and said, "Well, hello there. Is there something I can do for you?"

"No, I was just noticing your necklace. My mother has one just like it. She loves hers. Do you like yours?"

"Yes I do, honey," the woman patted Will on the shoulder and smiled. Will looked back at the ticket counter. The man was busy with another customer. Smiling at the woman, Will walked toward the small restaurant at the side of the terminal.

Going into the restaurant, Will sat on a stool at the counter. A young woman, her hair pinned back and dressed in a green checked uniform, walked up to Will. She got out her order pad and said. "What'll you have, sonny?"

"Just a glass of water," Will answered.

With a sigh, the woman put her pad back in her pocket and her pencil behind her ear. She brought back a glass of water and set it in front of Will. "Anything else I can do for you?" she asked.

"Yes, can I get some bills from you?"

"What are you talking about, kid?"

"I have a lot of change in my pocket and it's heavy. Could you give me some paper money for it?"

"Oh, sure, how much you got?"

Will reached down in his pocket and produced several handfuls of money. He removed the wrinkled bills and shoved them back into his pocket. Then he counted out two quarters and five dimes and put that in his pocket as well.

"We can always use change around here," the woman said as she began counting the pile of change. "Mildred," she yelled over her shoulder, "you take care of the customers for a minute. I have to help this young man."

At last she stood back. "I got $97.01. Is that what you got?"

Will was sure he had $98.52 in coins but that was before he bought the candy bar and had just now removed a dollar in change. He must have lost a penny somewhere but that was okay so he nodded his head.

The woman left his change on the counter while she went to the register. She came back with four twenties, one ten, one five, and two ones. Pushing one penny back at Will, she counted out the bills for him. She then scooped the coins into a bowl and returned to the register.

"Thanks a lot," Will said getting off the stool. He headed back into the terminal and noticed that a different man was now selling tickets. He went back to get in line. Only one person was ahead of him and soon Will asked the agent for a one way ticket to Dallas.

"That'll be $122.40. Who are you with, boy?"

"That's my mom, right back there," Will said as he waved at the woman. She smiled and waved back. "She thought she bought two tickets but she only has one. Here is my money." Will counted out the exact amount. Taking the ticket, Will walked over to the heavy set woman and sat down beside her.

"Where are you going, sweetheart," she asked him.

"Dallas," Will replied.

"Well, I am too. Are you on the bus that leaves at 10:40?"

"Yes, ma'am."

"Well, isn't that nice. Is your mother with you?"

"No, I'm going alone. My father is already there. I go to visit him often," Will said.

"Is your father expecting you?"

109

"No. I'm going to surprise him."

"Well, you'd better stay by me. You can't trust people these days. My name is Susie. What's yours?"

"My name is Luke," Will stretched the truth giving her his middle name.

Will sat next to Susie for almost an hour waiting for their bus to come in. Susie fell asleep waiting and awoke with a start each time the intercom burst forth with a static voice announcing arrivals and departures.

"All aboard for Bus Number 124, destined for South Bend, Indianapolis, Louisville, Memphis, Little Rock, Dallas and Fort Worth from Gate Number Seven."

"That's our bus, sweetie," Susie said, getting up and grabbing her very large purse.

Will and Susie climbed on the bus behind a long line of people boarding. There was no empty seat for the two of them. Susie sat with another lady and Will sat behind her with a man in military uniform.

The bus ride was quiet as they sped along. Will was thrilled that he was able to pull this off so

110

well. He was excited about seeing his dad once
again and was pretty sure his dad could talk his
mother into letting him stay at least until fall.
Maybe he could live with his father forever!

In Centerville, David wondered about Will.
He had not shown up all day. After school, David
went to the offices of The Detective Company
but today he couldn't get excited about what the
others were investigating. He kept thinking about
his pal. He always wished that Will was a member
of this exciting club. But Will had other things on
his mind like making a scrapbook with pictures of
motorcycles.

On his way home, David thought about
stopping at Will's house to see how he was, but
decided that may make Will's mother angry so he
went on home. Obviously, Will stayed home
today. He probably told his mother he was sick.
After David got done with his chores, it was supper
time and as soon as the dishwasher was loaded, he
planned to call Will.

111

But Will's mother called their house first. "Is Will at your house?" asked Mrs. Parker. Mrs. Mason turned from the phone and asked David, "Did Will say anything about going anywhere after school?"

David's stomach seemed to drop down to his feet. He went to his mother's side and asked, "Is Will in trouble?"

"No, David, his mother is looking for him. He did not come home from school this afternoon."

"I don't know where he is," David said, looking down at the floor.

After his mother had hung up the phone, David looked up at her and said, "Mom, Will did not come to school today."

"What? Do you know where he is?"

"No, Mom. We walked to school but just as we came out of the woods, he remembered he had left his map at home and ran back to get it. I thought he had decided to stay home."

The bus was slowing down.

112

"Luke," Susie called from the seat in front of Will.

"Luke," she called again.

The bus was pulling into the parking lot of a restaurant and people began to get off the bus. "Luke, have you been sleeping?" Susie asked.

"Oh, yeah," Will replied. "Were you calling me?"

"Yes. You need to get out and walk around a bit. You have not gotten off this bus all day. Aren't you hungry or anything?"

I don't want to get off and miss getting back on."

"They announce when our bus is leaving. You won't miss it, I promise."

"Okay." Will got off and ordered an egg salad sandwich and a glass of water at the lunch counter. He didn't know how much money he may need when he got to Dallas. He may need to take a cab to his dad's house and his money was running low. Will knew he had better spend as little money as possible.

Getting back on the bus, Will was thrilled when the soldier did not return. Will hoped he

113

would continue to have the seat to himself. It was dark now. Will stretched out on the seat and slept.

The phone rang once again at David's house. David was getting ready for bed and his mother came in to see him after she had hung up the phone.

"Will's mother is very upset. He is still missing. Do you have any idea in the world where he could be?"

"Mom, Will hasn't been happy at home since his parents got a divorce. He'll probably go home when he gets hungry."

"For pity's sake, David. I hope you never pull a stunt like this. His mother is sick with worry. Her husband has called the police and they are trying to figure out where he may have gone. Do you know where he liked to hide or if anyone would help him if he asked?"

"He would have asked me, Mom. I'm his best friend."

"I'll tell your father to look in our garage and

I'll look down the basement. Maybe he is hiding somewhere here."

Mrs. Mason left David standing in his room wearing his pajama pants and holding his pajama top. David could envision Will sleeping in a tree in the woods. He wished Will would knock on his door right now. He looked under his bed and in his closet. Where could he be? David didn't think Will would run away without telling him.

Will woke up with a start, forgetting for a moment where he was. Susie was asleep in the seat in front of him. Anxiously he looked for some sign of where they were. But in the darkness, he could only see scattered lights of homes as the bus rolled along. Suddenly the headlights of the bus illuminated a sign "Welcome to Texas" and Will felt safe and happy.

115

He turned on the overhead light and looked through his magazine one more time. It was about motorcycles and Will dreamed of the day he would own one.

In Centerville, Mrs. Mason turned on the TV just as David came down the next morning. He was dressed for school. As the news commentator talked, the two of them stood transfixed with what was being reported. "A Centerville youth has been reported missing since sometime yesterday. He was last seen wearing a blue and white striped T-shirt and blue jeans. He is 13 years old, is approximately 5 feet tall and has blond wavy hair. This is a recent photo of the boy, William Gooding. He lives with his mother and stepfather, the Parkers. The family is asking anyone with any knowledge of his whereabouts to please call the Centerville Police."

As daylight came to the Texas plains, Will could see fenced in fields with cattle grazing. He got out his comb and tried to make his hair neat although he had no mirror to use. At last they came into the big city; the tall buildings thrilled Will as they always did.

After what seemed eons, the bus finally rolled into the terminal. Will got off, carrying his book bag. Susie's friend had come to meet her. "You have a nice time at your dad's," she called with a wave. Will smiled and waved farewell.

Going into the station and using a pay phone, he dialed his dad's phone number that he knew by heart. Before the phone rang, Will hung up. It would be better to talk to his dad face to face.

He went outside and found a long line of taxicabs waiting for a fare. He got into the one at the head of the line and told the driver his dad's address. The driver said nothing on the trip into the suburbs until they were pulling in front of the house. "You live here?"

"Yeah," Will answered.

"$8.50."

Will carefully counted out the exact amount

117

and handed it to the driver. The driver looked a bit disappointed but shrugged his shoulders as Will got out of the vehicle. Will headed up the driveway toward the back door. Passing by the kitchen window, he saw Diana working in the kitchen.

Ducking down, Will had to make a decision. He knew his dad's girlfriend, Diana. With a sigh, he decided that they must have gotten married like his dad had told him that they may. Diana was okay but he was sure she would insist that Will return to his mother until his appointed time to stay with them. Moving stealthily, Will went behind the house and entered the garage through the door on the side.

His father's new car stood shining in the dim light and the old car that his family had owned since he was born stood beside it. Will got into the old car and sat in the back seat, quietly closing the car door. The smell of leather and cigarette smoke was familiar. He was not sure of what to do. He waited quietly, hoping he could catch his dad alone and talk to him.

It wasn't long until Will heard them talking outside. Will got down on the floor to hide as the big door of the garage swung open. His dad opened the trunk of the new car and after several thumping sounds, the trunk was slammed shut.

"They will have our plane tickets ready to pick up when we get to the airport," Will heard Diana say as she got into the new car. The car doors slammed and Will kept hiding while his father drove from the garage and then got out to shut the big door of the garage. Will waited in the darkness for several minutes just in case they returned.

When all remained quiet, Will got out of the car. He peeked out of the window and was relieved to see that all was still outside and there was no one in sight. He came out of the garage and tried to open the side door of the house. It was locked. He looked in the flower pot by the door and found the key where his dad kept it.

Will opened the door of the house and went in. The smell of toast still lingered in the air but the

119

kitchen had been cleaned up and there was no sign of habitation. Will opened the refrigerator and found eggs, lunch meat, cheese and milk, along with the usual condiments. The freezer was full of wonderful things that were easy to fix.

Will walked into the living room and turned on the TV. He immediately turned it to his favorite channel. A veterinarian was operating on a parrot.

Will had gotten very little rest on the bus. He looked in the room where he stayed when he lived with his dad. The bed was made up but when Will pulled down the bedspread to get a pillow, he found there was no pillowcase nor sheets on the bed. He took the pillow out to the living room and made himself comfortable on the couch. Watching the procedure of the vet lulled Will to asleep.

The Centerville Middle School lunchroom had the usual volume of voices raised during this free time when students were able to talk and get away from their studies. David sat with Tom and

Ben. "Where's your shadow," Tom teased David.

"I really don't know," David answered. "He has been missing since yesterday. His mother has called the police and everything!"

"He probably ran away to join the circus," Tom said with a serious face but then broke into a grin. "He'll be Willie the Clown."

"Come on, Tom," Ben said, elbowing his buddy. "This could be serious."

"Well, then, let's take it to The Detective Company."

"I don't know if we would be any help. The police are already working on it," David said.

"Tom's right," Ben said. "We've solved things for the police before."

"Okay," David said, "I will bring **The Case of the Missing Teen** to The Detective Company at tonight's meeting."

When Will woke up, a show was featuring the cocker spaniel. He got up and went into the kitchen. Opening the freezer, he spied a pizza and followed the directions to bake it in the oven. He poured himself a glass of cola and went back into the living room to perch on the couch. Since Will was a fan of hound dogs, he switched the channel to the game shows.

Soon he could smell something burning and ran into the kitchen to remove a very black pizza from the oven. He turned off the oven and got out a carton of ice cream instead. He took the lid off, got a spoon from the drawer and carried the carton into the living room. Sitting down, he began surfing the channels. News was always boring so he skipped on past and found a good action film featuring dirt bikes.

Will thought about calling his best friend, David, but decided that would be foolish. David's mother may intervene and tell David to report Will's whereabouts to his mother. Right now, Will was enjoying the peace of being alone and having no rules to follow.

The CMS last bell had rung and students were exiting the school building or going to different areas for extra activities. David put his book bag in his locker and headed for The Detective Company offices.

Maggie McMillan was already in the room and had rolled her wheel chair over to the spot where the members always gathered around her for the meeting.

"Okay, we have several cases going on right now. Who would like to be the first to report?"

David raised his hand. "I don't have a case right now, Maggie, but I would like to tell everyone about my missing friend."

"Go ahead, David," Maggie said.

"My best friend and I were walking to school yesterday morning when he remembered he had forgotten his homework. He told me he would see me in school and then ran back toward his house. He never came to school and his mother called our house two times last night trying to find him."

"Is your friend's name, Will Gooding?" Maggie asked.

"Yes! Did they find him?"

123

"No, David. But it has been on the news."

"Maybe someone kidnapped him," Nick said.

"Maybe he ran away," Hannah suggested.

"Will told me that he thought his mother and stepfather didn't like him living there," David said quietly.

"He may have moved into a cardboard box to become a homeless kid," suggested Katie.

"He may be dead," Sharon shouted.

"Everyone calm down," Maggie said. "The police have already been searching the area and have a few clues. You people are Will's age. Think about where you might go if you were angry with your parents. This is The Detective Company. What can you do to help in this case?"

"We could search the woods and around the neighborhood where Will might have gone. Is the circus in town?" Tom asked with a grin, but no one laughed.

"How about if we talked to all our friends that may know Will," Ben suggested. "Perhaps they could give us a clue."

"We could look in his room for clues!" stated Nick.

"These are all good suggestions," Maggie said. "However, I doubt if the police will allow anyone into the house. If there is any evidence, they would not want it disturbed.

"I plan to be here again tomorrow," Maggie continued. " so if there are no objections we will put all other cases on hold for today. I suggest you go out in groups of three or four to investigate. Meet me back here in an hour to report."

Three teams of investigators left the building right away. Bree, Tom and Hannah, with her seeing-eye dog, went off to the woods. Jack, David and Nick walked downtown to the drugstore and dollar store. Drew, Ben, Sharon and Katie, on her wheels, went out to the ball field to talk to students there.

The woods had already been searched thoroughly by the police. Hannah stopped when her dog indicated a root was in the path. Stopping to wait for her to find the obstacle with her foot, Bree noticed a penny on the ground.

"I wonder if this has any meaning?"

125

Showing the coin to Tom, she then placed it in Hannah's hand. "It may not mean anything, but let's take it back with us," Bree told them.

At the drug store, Nick asked the woman at the counter if she had seen a boy their age in the store yesterday. She told them that she had not, but the owner had told the police a boy had been in the drug store early that morning and bought a magazine to take on a class trip. Nick, David and Jack exchanged glances. Could that have been Will?

Out on the playing field, Drew, Ben, Sharon and Katie split up to talk to different groups about their missing classmate. No one seemed to have any information to share. As they regrouped to head back to the school, one of the members of the soccer team ran over to talk to them.

"Are you asking about the missing boy named Will?" the student panted from running.

"Yes," answered Sharon.

"Why are you asking about this?"

"We are members of The Detective Company," explained Drew.

"Oh, yes, I should have known," the student

replied. "My name is Rachel. I was late coming to school yesterday morning. My mother brought me in the car. As we passed the woods across from the school, I saw a young person leaning against a tree in the woods. I wondered why he was there. I think it was a boy."

"Thank you for your help," Ben said.

With a wave, Rachel ran back to her team-mates.

Will was getting bored sitting in his dad's house but he dared not go out as one of the neighbors might see him. He turned off the TV and looked in the freezer for something to eat. Choosing a pot pie, he read the directions to cook it in the microwave and was soon enjoying a warm supper.

Going upstairs to his dad's bedroom, he found a computer had been installed on a desk. Having experience with computers from school, he turned on the machine and waited for it to warm up. He got up and looked in the closet and found that half of the closet was filled with women's clothing. He was disappointed to realize that his father had remarried. Diana was okay but he was sure his dad would no longer have as much time for him as he had in the past summers. He may not be wanted in this house either.

Back in Centerville, David walked home after The Detective Company had summed up their findings thus far. He was upset with his friend's disappearance. Coming into the house, he called to his mother who came dashing from the kitchen to greet him. She hugged him and then asked him about his day.

"The Detective Company is trying to find out what has happened to Will. We did some investigating but didn't find out very much."

"I have been listening to the news, David, and I have talked with some of our neighbors. The police found blood in Will's room and are investigating the possibility of kidnapping. Will's own father and his new stepmother flew in this morning to be with the family. We can only hope that Will is all right and will be found soon."

David's family drove down to the local fast food restaurant for dinner to break the gloom that had settled in the house. But even there, people were talking about the tragedy at the Parker home and shared their thoughts of what might have happened. Questions were raised if old refrigerators and trunks had been searched. Had everyone looked in their own basements to see if he was hiding there. No one had heard if the family had been contacted by a kidnapper.

That night David was still thinking about Will as he fell asleep.

The time in Texas was one hour earlier and the computer chirped a friendly beep as Will found a wonderful game already installed. Losing all track of time, Will played on the computer for hours. He turned on no lights as the screen provided light from within and he continued to play far into the night. At last he laid down on his father's bed and fell fast asleep.

As David awoke, his first thought was of his friend. It was Saturday morning and it was a pretty day outside. He wished that Will was at home even if he could not come out to goof off today.

He went down to the kitchen for breakfast and found his mother making pancakes. "How does a boy disappear when he has no money?" she asked David.

David thought about this and recalled where Will kept his secret horde of money that he was saving to buy a computer. David jumped up and said, "Mom, I need to see Mrs. Parker."

"You shouldn't bother her, David. The news this morning reported that Will is still missing. His mother must be heartbroken."

"No, Mom! I may be able to help her."

With a startled look, his mother watched him run out the door and through the back yard. Running up to Will's house, David pounded on the door. Will's stepfather came to the door. "Go away. We want no visitors today. Please leave us alone."

"Wait! I think I can help you find Will."

Will's mother came to the door and asked David to come in. "How can you help us?" she said, wringing her hands.

"I need to look in Will's room." David said.

"David, this is Officer Bird." Mrs. Parker said, putting her arm around David. "He is keeping everyone out of Will's room. Officer, this is Will's best friend, David."

The officer shook David's hand and told him they would greatly appreciate any help he could give them. The two walked down the hall and David saw that they had taped off Will's room. Everything had been picked up and the room was straightened.

"Will didn't keep his room this neat," David said.

"We have carefully examined everything in here. Then we put things away to make getting around in the room easier. See where we dusted for fingerprints? You may go in, but don't touch anything."

131

Ducking under the yellow tape, David walked into the room. He reached for a book in the bookcase.

"Hold on there. What are you doing?" asked the officer.

"I need to look in one book," David explained.

When Officer Bird gestured to go ahead, David took out the volume of *Tom Sawyer* and opened it, looking through the pages.

"What is it, son?"

"There should be a key in here."

Just then a key fell on the floor. Picking it up, David told the officer to get the metal box from the shelf in the closet. The officer took the box from the shelf and David saw that the lock had been broken.

"What happened?"

"We had to open that when we were searching for clues," the officer replied.

David opened the box and looked inside. "Is this what you found in here?"

"Yes, we put the papers back in just like we found them."

David saw the map that Will had drawn that last night they had done homework together. He knew that there should be a lot of money in the box.

"Wasn't there some money in here?"

The officer shook his head and answered. "Only the papers."

David got up and opened the desk drawer. He took out a small notebook and opened it.

"What have you got there, David? We thought that was Will's address book."

"It is. May I call this number?"

The officer led David back into the living room. David saw a strange man and woman in the room. The man stood up and said, "Hello David. Will has told me so much about you. I'm Will's father, Bill Gooding and this is my wife Diana."

David smiled at them and then turned to the officer. "I still need to call this number. It is Will's father's phone number in Texas. Even though Mr. Gooding is here, Will may be hiding in his father's home."

"What?" Will's father jumped up. "Here, I will call on my cell phone."

The number was dialed and while everyone waited, Mr. Gooding listened. He then said, "Will, are you there? Pick up the phone, Will."

He finally hung up the phone and said, "That was an excellent idea but he is not there."

David sat down and told the adults his summation of the case.

"I am a member of The Detective Company at Centerville Middle School. Our group has been investigating this case. I know that Will had a lot of money in his strong box that he was saving for a computer. I'm sure he had enough money saved to buy a bus ticket to Dallas. He left me on the way to school Thursday morning to go back for his homework. I just now found that homework in his strong box and the money he had saved is gone.

"A student told The Detective Company that

she saw a boy hiding in the woods while her mother was driving her to school. She was late that morning so when she saw the person, it was after first hour had started.

"Plus, the owner of the drugstore downtown sold a magazine yesterday morning to someone that could be Will. The drug store is just around the corner from the bus station. I think that Will bought a bus ticket to go to see his dad and must have missed him. Does he know how to get into your house, Mr. Gooding?"

"Well, yes, he knows where I keep a key outside the house."

"May we call the house again? This time I will talk."

Mr. Gooding hit the re-dial and handed his phone to David.

Once again the phone rang and David talked to the answering machine. "Will, it's David. Answer the phone, Will. The entire town is looking for you and some people think you are either kidnapped or dead. Your folks are very sad." When there was still no answer, David sighed and gave the phone back to Mr. Gooding.

"I'm sorry, everybody. I thought that Will may have gotten to Texas. I'll let myself out."

After the officer and the family thanked him for his effort. David walked slowly back to his house.

Will woke up to the sound of the phone ringing. He laid there and the ringing soon stopped. He was hungry and decided to see what he could find in the freezer for breakfast. As he came down the stairs, the phone began ringing again. He stopped and listened as his dad's recorded voice told the caller to leave a message.

"Will, it's David. Answer the phone, Will." Will stood very still listening and then ran to the phone. He saw the number of where the call was coming from on the caller ID screen. "The entire town is looking for you and some people think you are either kidnapped or dead. Your folks are very sad." Will could see that David was calling from a familar numer. It wasWill's father's cell phone!

Will went into the living room and turned on

the TV. He switched to the national news station and watched as his mother, his stepfather and his own father were talking to the commentator about him! His mother was crying and both his father and stepfather looked very worried. The commentator said the investigation had shown that Will may have been kidnapped from his room as there was unexplained blood on his bed. However, there were several witnesses that said he had left for school that morning.

Will sat down on the couch, stunned. He had not realized that his mother and stepfather would even care if he was missing. And now he knew why his father and his new wife had taken a plane yesterday morning. They had gone to be with his mother and stepfather.

Will went to the phone and called David's house. Mrs. Mason answered the phone. "Hello."

"May I speak to David, please."

"He's not home right now. Will, is that you? Wait a minute. David just came in."

"David, it's for you. It sounds like Will."

David took the phone. "Hello."

"David, I'm in Texas. I listened to you talk

on the phone but I was afraid to answer. Am I in a lot of trouble?"

"Will! Your folks will be so glad that you are okay. Let me go over and tell them."

"No. I will call them, David. I never knew that I would be missed at my house."

That afternoon, Will's father arranged for him to fly back to Centerville. Will had flown often in summer's past. He received a warm welcome from his four parents. They were all delighted to see him safe. Both of his stepparents gave him warm hugs. Will and his two sets of parents spent the afternoon talking. Everyone vowed to work together to make a better family.

On Monday afternoon, David came into The Detective Company offices and was met by loud cheering and clapping.

"David, you did it! You solved the case

while the rest of us were watching Saturday TV or cleaning our rooms!" Katie announced, twisting a curl in her hair.

David grinned. He had spent a while with Will on Sunday afternoon and heard all about his adventure to Dallas and how surprised Will was to find that all his family loved him, including his stepfather.

"I used all the deductive reasoning we learned here together. It was a thing that needed to be done immediately. I wish I could have shared more of it with you," David told them. "The best thing is that Will is very glad to be back home."

The End

The Case of the Vanishing Tennis Balls

"Listen up!" yelled Mr. Wilson, the Centerville High School Tennis Coach. His players grouped around him. "Okay, I've got 100 brand new tennis balls and these need to last for the entire season. So let's keep track of them, got it?"

"Got it, Coach," the team yelled in unison. Then as a hush fell, Ted Gibbons muttered, "These will probably have most of the fuzz off of them in a couple of weeks."

"Good," Coach Wilson replied, "That means you are practicing hard and that is the only way we can win. I'm not concerned with how many times you hit the ball but how well you hit it. Just don't lose them. Okay? It's vital we get them to last for the season. Is everyone with me?"

"Got it, Coach," the team yelled again.

"Hit 'em but don't lose 'em!" Lori Leskey added.

"Exactly. Don't lose any balls. We've got matches against Middleton and River Heights in the next week. Get back to the courts. You all need to work on your serves and forehands."

"Coach, don't forget the bubble gum," said Eric Bastain, the team captain. "We need something to work off our tension. Especially after the matches. We've got to have that gum and lots of it."

"Yeah, I'll get it," the coach said. "I'll pass it out after your matches."

The practice was a good one. The players continued to sharpen their skills and it looked like the Centerville Spartans might beat their rivals, the Middleton Hornets. Perhaps the River Heights Bulldogs would fall victim as well.

The day of the first match arrived. The Centerville school bus pulled up at the site of the tennis match. The players got off the bus proudly carrying their rackets and the bag of 100 balls. To safe-guard their return, the balls each were imprinted with a CHS stamp.

The Spartan tennis team turned serious and went through pre-game exercises. With an occasional glance at the opposing team, they sized up their competition. As they completed their routine, the Centerville coach shouted, "Listen up!"

145

Encircling the coach, they heard his questions. "Everybody ready to go? Are you warmed up? Ready to win?"

"Let's go, Spartans!" they shouted.

The Spartans played exceptionally well on the warm afternoon. They fell behind early in the match, but rallied and won. This victory was huge. The team felt great and was ready to celebrate all the way back to Centerville.

"Hey, Coach, may we have our victory gum?" Captain Bastain asked as he boarded the bus. "Our mouths are pretty dry and the tension has been fierce."

"Sure," the coach handed the bubble gum to the team manager Betsy Batway and told her to see that everyone got a six-piece package of gum.

Moving down the road, the team was busy chewing and patting each other on the back, celebrating their win. As the bus entered the city limits of Centerville, the coach reached for the ball bag and counted the balls. He could only come up with 88.

"Listen up, Spartans," he yelled. Everything got quiet on the bus to listen to the coach. "There

146

are twelve tennis balls missing!"

"We're bound to lose a few," the team captain replied.

"Yes, but we've lost twelve! We can't have that for every match or we'll not make it through the season. What happened to them? Any idea?"

"I don't know. I didn't see anyone take them," Lisa Jefferies said.

"Neither did I and I was trying to pay attention," said the team manager.

The question left everyone quiet until the bus pulled into the school driveway. What could have happened to twelve tennis balls?

Before the team got off the bus to be greeted by friends and parents, the coach stood at the front of the bus and faced the team. "We need everyone to be on guard here. We've got to find those missing balls. Keep your eyes and ears open and report anything suspicious to me."

"Got it, Coach," the team yelled as they stood to get off the bus.

The week passed without further incident. No more balls were missing but the twelve had not been found either. At the next meet the team played successfully at home against the Bulldogs and the tennis ball count remained at 88 at the end of the meet.

The third meet was approaching and it was against the Aggies from Oakdale. This would be a road trip so off the team went with 88 tennis balls. After the match, won by Centerville, the members of the team collected the tennis balls, got their victory gum and headed down the road back home. Getting close to town, Coach Wilson counted the tennis balls and once again more balls were missing. Now the number was down to 64.

Coach shouted above the noise of the bus at the celebrating tennis players. "Listen up! We've lost 24 more tennis balls! What is going on here? If we don't solve this problem, we'll not be the State champs that you so much want to be. We have to find those balls or we're going to be all washed up!"

The team was quiet as they filed off the bus. Some of them patted the coach as they passed, hoping to raise his spirits.

That evening at dinner, Rich Ancil, a Centerville High School student and a fan of the tennis team, shared with his family the story of the tennis balls missing after an away match.

His little sister, Hannah, listened with interest. Hannah is blind from birth but able to attend school with non-handicapped children her own age. "Are you saying, the balls only disappear when the team is visiting another school for a match?" she asked her brother.

"That's right," he admitted.

"This sounds like a case for The Detective Company," said Hannah. "May I take this to my meeting tomorrow?"

"Oh, sure," Rich said with a chuckle. "Do you think you and your members could solve this mystery?"

"We could certainly try. We have a meeting tomorrow afternoon and I will present the case to them." Smiling happily, Hannah finished her dinner with Rich and their parents.

149

The next day as the Spartan tennis team took to their courts to practice, The Detective Company was beginning their meeting at the Centerville Middle School.   The students gathered around Maggie McMillan. She is a renowned detective in Centerville and a volunteer in guiding The Detective Company in solving cases at the school and the surrounding community.

Taking turns, students reported on the progress of cases presently under their investigation. As always, suggestions poured from members and the ideas were usually good ones; sometimes impossible and other times very workable for this age group.

When Maggie asked the group if there were any new cases developing, Hannah raised her hand. Hannah always manned the phones at the office of The Detective Company and was popular with all the members.

"Hannah, have you been bothered by a crank caller?" teased Tom, the group's comedian. "Or maybe you have found a wire tap on our phone."

"No, it's nothing like that." Hannah declared. "The high school tennis team is having a problem with their tennis balls. Someone is taking them when they go on a road trip."

"It must be the other team," said Sharon. "They would want the balls to use themselves."

"The balls are marked with the initials of Centerville High School," Hannah replied. "My brother told me that each one has CHS imprinted on it."

"Well, that could be covered up with a felt tip pen," suggested Jack.

"I'm sure that the coach has thought of that and inquired at the school where they played. Tennis balls with big black marks on them would be pretty obvious," replied Hannah.

"Well, Hannah, it sounds like you have given this some thought," said Maggie. "Does anyone have any idea of what could have happened to the tennis balls? Why would anyone want tennis balls other than to play tennis?"

"I know that the third grade room at the elementary school has tennis balls on the feet of their desk chairs." said Drew, who wears a hearing aid. "There are two hearing impaired children in the room and the noise of the chairs scraping the floor is loud and distracting for anyone wearing a hearing aid. My little sister is in that room and she told me about their cutting an "x" in tennis balls so they could be placed on the feet of the chairs. That stops the sound of the scraping."

The Detective Company became quiet as they envisioned a classroom with four tennis balls on each desk chair. "That would take a lot of tennis balls," said Katie, tossing her curls and getting a brush from her purse that hung from the arm of her chair.

"Do you know the name of your sister's teacher?" Maggie asked Drew.

"Yes, it's Mrs. Snow," replied Drew.

"I will call her right now," said Maggie. "She may be still at the school." The members sat quietly while Maggie rolled her wheelchair over to the phone to place the call. "Mrs. Snow, please," said Maggie and then sat smiling at them as they waited expectantly.

"Mrs. Snow, it's Maggie McMillan. I work with The Detective Company over at the middle school."

After a pause, Maggie said, "Oh yes, I do recall meeting you at the Teachers' Gathering at the beginning of school this year. Well, we need your help today as we are investigating why tennis balls are missing at the high school."

Again after a pause, Maggie continued, "We have learned that the desk chairs in your classroom have tennis balls on them. May I ask where you got them?"

After a long pause, Maggie said, "Well, that explains your having all those tennis balls. It does not help us solve our case but it certainly explains to us where you got the balls. Thank you, Mrs. Snow."

Hanging up the phone and rolling back to the group, Maggie told them, "One of Mrs. Snow's hearing impaired students had visited a grandmother in a nursing home and seen that they used tennis balls on the walkers to quiet the noise of the walker feet. The sound of chairs scraping on the floor of a classroom causes problems for those who

153

wear hearing aids. The noise of the chairs is amplified and distorts the sounds the children should hear.

"Mrs. Snow called the nursing home to find out where they had gotten their tennis balls and was told who to contact" continued Maggie. "Mrs. Snow's class wrote to the tennis ball company explaining their need for 96 tennis balls. The tennis ball company sent ball 'seconds', or tennis balls that did not meet their standards, to Mrs. Snow's class."

"Well, that was a dead-end clue," said Nick. "What else can you do with tennis balls besides play tennis?"

The room was quiet as members thought about this mystery. "Well, Hannah, it looks like you have a true mystery to solve. Does anyone have any ideas of what Hannah should do?"

"She should talk to the tennis coach and the players too," said Bree, tossing her long braid from her shoulder.

"Yeah, and talk to the remaining tennis balls, too," kidded Tom.

The group laughed at Tom's joke and then

turned serious once more. "Maybe it would help if we knew what the balls looked like," suggested David. "Tennis balls come in different colors and maybe that would help identify them. That is something you can ask the coach."

Hannah thanked the members for their help and set to work making a plan of how to address the problem of solving **The Case of the Vanishing Tennis Balls**.

The next day, Hannah walked over to the high school after her own school had let out for the day. She has a seeing-eye dog named Mellow that she had gotten when she entered middle school. Her dog is a golden retriever and her constant companion. All the students at the school had learned that they must not approach Mellow when he was in his harness, because he was working and should not be distracted.

Today Mellow walked calmly at Hannah's right side, gently but firmly guiding her along the sidewalk. Her best friend Bree tagged along to show the way. The high school was located just half a block from the middle school and the tennis courts were behind the gymnasium.

Approaching Coach Wilson, who was standing with his arms folded watching his team practice, Bree touched his arm and gestured toward Hannah. Looking at the blind girl with her dog, the coach said, "Well, well, what can I do for you young ladies?"

"Hello, Coach. My name is Hannah and this is my partner Bree. We are here from The Detective Company," said Hannah boldly. "We are investigating your vanishing tennis balls and would like to help you."

Frowning, the coach asked, "Just what do you think you can do to help us?"

"May we ask you some questions?" queried Hannah.

"Sure. Go ahead," said Coach Wilson.

"Can you tell us what the tennis balls that are missing look like?"

"Hey, Lisa," shouted the coach, making Hannah jump as he yelled. "Bring me a ball over here."

156

Lisa came running over and tossed a ball to the coach.

"Okay, get back to your practice," said the coach and turned to Hannah. "Here is what they look like."

"May I hold it?" asked Hannah.

"Oh, sure," replied the coach, embarrassed at his own lack of sensitivity. He handed the ball to Hannah who felt its rough texture. She turned to Bree and asked her about the ball.

"It is bright green and has CHS stamped on it," said Bree.

157

"May we keep it?" asked Hannah.

"Oh my, no," said the coach. "We already have too many balls missing, I can't have another one gone."

"We will bring it back in a day or two," said Hannah. "I want to share its appearance with the members of The Detective Company. I promise I won't let anything happen to it."

"I'm sorry," said Coach Wilson with determination. "I can't allow any more of our balls to disappear."

"Well, can you tell us when you notice that the balls are missing?" Hannah asked.

"It's right after we have had a match on the road," replied the coach.

"On the road?" asked Hannah. "I don't understand."

"I mean when we are playing a match at another school. When we play at home at our school, the balls don't disappear."

"And you don't have reason to believe that the balls are stolen by the opposing team?" asked Bree.

"No. That was my first suspicion but the

coaches of both schools where we had later found
we had balls missing assured me that their
members use only white balls. Their team
members have not seen any green balls among their
equipment. And we have our initials on every
ball."

"Could we talk to one of your team
members?" asked Hannah.

"Hey, Eric," shouted Coach Wilson, causing
Hannah to cringe again. "Come over here on the
double."

A young athlete ran over to the girls and
looked expectantly at the coach. "Girls, this is Eric
Bastain, our team captain. Eric, this is Hannah and
Bree from the middle school detective group," said
the coach. "They are investigating our vanishing
balls mystery."

The girls stood quietly beside Eric and his
coach. "May we speak to Eric alone?" asked
Hannah.

"Oh, I'm sorry. I didn't mean to get in the
way of your investigation," said the coach walking
away.

"Eric, do have any idea what has been

happening to your tennis balls?" asked Hannah.

"I haven't a clue," said Eric with a grin. "Coach is getting all uptight about a minor problem. I wouldn't waste my time on this if I were you."

"Why is he so concerned while you are not?" asked Bree.

"Oh, I'm concerned but they'll probably turn up sooner or later," said Eric. "I don't know why he gets so bent out of shape over such a trivial problem. One of the parents will probably donate more balls if the missing ones aren't found."

"Thank you for your help," said Hannah.

Turning, the girls and Hannah's big dog headed back toward the gymnasium and the sidewalk to the middle school.

"What did you think of what they told us," Bree asked Hannah.

"Well, I think the coach is finding it much more serious than the team; at least the team captain doesn't seem so serious about it."

"Could you tell he was smiling?" asked Bree.

"Oh yes, people talk differently when they are smiling," Hannah told her stopping to face

Bree. "People breathe out while they talk and the breath often comes out in a rush when they have something funny to say."

"Do you think the captain or some of the players know something about all of this?" asked Bree.

"I don't know, but it is a possibility. Maybe I should go to the next out of town match," said Hannah as she took off her sunglasses, got a handkerchief from her pocket and began to wipe them.

"Why do you do that?" asked Bree.

"I often hear people talk about how dirty their glasses are," confessed Hannah. "I just want to be sure my glasses look clean."

"They look clean to me," said Bree with a smile and then added, "Will you take Maggie with you to the match?"

"I hope she can go," answered Hannah.

At the next meeting of The Detective Company, Hannah reported on all that had transpired at the tennis courts and gave them a description of the tennis balls. She told of her plan to attend the next out of town match that was with

161

Pine Grove. Nick suggested that someone from
their group go with Hannah to watch carefully what
happened.

"Would you be interested in going with
Hannah?" asked Maggie.

"Boy, would I!" replied Nick.

"Perhaps four eyes would be better than two;
so Hannah has a good description of what is going
on," suggested Bree. "I would be willing to go
along too."

"Great," said Maggie. "I will arrange with
Coach Martin for the three of you to attend the next
match. Perhaps I can convince him to allow you
on the players' bus and I can follow in my van."

"That would be wonderful," said Hannah.
"We would be able to know everything that goes on
if we travel with the team!"

The morning of the next road trip arrived
with The Detective Company having permission to
ride with the team to the scheduled match. As
Nick, Bree, Hannah and Mellow climbed the steps

to the bus, the coach told them to sit on the two seats next to the bus door. Bree and Nick took the front seat. Hannah and Mellow sat behind them.

Mellow immediately laid down on the floor on Hannah's feet. Bree checked for Hannah to be sure that Mellow did not block the aisle as the dog was almost as long as the space in front of the seat.

The players began to come onto the bus and with raised eyebrows, looked at the detectives. When everyone was seated, Coach Wilson stood up from his seat across the aisle from the detectives and introduced the threesome as students from the middle school who were going to investigate the mystery of the vanishing tennis balls. The players, who were sitting in pairs or alone on the remaining

163

seats of the bus, chuckled at the prospect of kids solving the coach's mystery.

Each player had their racket with them and a duffel bag. The bag of balls was on the floor right behind the coach, between the feet of Betsy, the team manager. Before the bus arrived at Pine Grove, the coach reached back to Betsy and took the bag of balls. He carefully counted and found that there were still 64 balls in the bag.

Returning the bag to the team manager, he stood and yelled, "Listen up!" Hannah jerked with the bellow of the coach's voice.

"Oh, I'm sorry," Coach Wilson said to Hannah, patting her shoulder.

Again turning up the volume of his voice, he told one and all that no more balls had better be missing on the trip home. He wished all the players good luck in their match against Pine Grove and they yelled "Let's go, Spartans!"

The players were polite as they waited for their guests to get off the bus first. With the assistance of Mellow, Hannah found her way down the bus steps. Maggie was waiting for them just outside.

Maggie and Hannah with her dog took seats at the bottom of the stands while Bree and Nick made their way to stand beside the bag of tennis balls. Their heads constantly moved as they watched all the people that came near the bag.

While the teams warmed up, Maggie told Hannah what was happening. "The team has a manager, Hannah. That person is a student who does not play tennis. She is in charge of the equipment and that includes the bag of tennis balls, a water cooler and a few extra rackets just in case they are needed.

"Bree and Nick have stationed themselves beside the bag of tennis balls," Maggie continued.

"Oh, I hope they will find a clue to the vanishing balls," cried Hannah.

During the match no one came close to the bag of balls except team members who needed a drink of water. Bree and Nick watched little of the match due to their constant alertness of anyone coming near the bag. In the meantime, Hannah was enjoying the solid sound of the balls as they hit the pavement of the court and could tell who had the advantage from whether the crowd cheered from her side of the courts or the other side.

At the end of the match, the Spartans all came to Betsy and gave her the balls they had been using. Bree and Nick then stood with Betsy as she carefully counted the balls in the bag. The count was still 64 and the detectives felt that their presence may have prevented any theft of the tennis balls. They ran alongside the team manager as she carried the bag of balls back to the bus. They watched her put the bag safely at her feet. Bree and Nick then reported to Hannah, who was already on the bus, that all was well with the count of tennis balls. That the number remained at 64.

Coach Wilson boarded the bus after all the players had gotten on. "Have you counted the balls, Betsy?" asked the coach.

"Yes, sir," Betsy said with a smile. "The count is 64!"

"Good job, Betsy!"

The Centerville Spartans had won the match against Pine Grove. The players chewed their victory bubble gum while singing the fight song with gusto. The Detective Company members soon caught on to the words of the tune and joined in the singing. As the bus neared Centerville, Coach Wilson took the bag of balls from the team manager and counted them.

"We're now down to 41 tennis balls!" the coach bellowed. "Stop your singing! We've got a major problem here! Someone is stealing our tennis balls!"

The bus continued on toward home with little sound from anyone on board. Bree and Nick looked at the players. They did not seem to feel as worried about the missing balls as the coach. They were looking out the bus windows or seemed to be sleeping. However, they were no longer joking with each other, singing, or bobbing up and down.

Earlier as they kept their eyes on the players, Bree and Nick had not been able to tell what the players had been doing when they would duck down in their seats. It appeared that they must be looking into their duffel bags or tying their shoes. But now the happy atmosphere of the win had turned into silence in respect for their coach's dismay.

When the bus slowed down to exit the highway, Hannah whispered to her co-detectives. "Hey!" The threesome huddled together to hear Hannah's question. "What is going on with the players?" They told her about the team's obvious reluctance to continue their celebration. However, the team seemed to still be in a much better mood than the coach.

"Did you notice anything else?" Hannah asked.

"Well, most of them have ducked down once or twice to get into their duffel bags or tie their shoes or something," said Bree. "But they don't get near the bag of tennis balls."

As the bus rolled to a stop, the coach stood and faced everyone on the bus. "Listen up! This has turned into a nightmare. The young students on this bus have been carefully watching every move of each player, the manager, the bus driver and me. And I doubt that they have come up with any answers. Have you, kids?"

Hannah raised her hand. "I would like you to check each person's duffel bag as they come to the front of the bus. Also, it would be best to check the racks above the seats and the floor. Even the water cooler and the bus driver's area should be examined. I think we may solve this mystery today."

Hannah's voice was loud and clear with resolve. Bree and Nick looked dubious but said nothing as they totally supported Hannah with her investigation.

"Well, the racks above the seats are just metal bars so I could see tennis balls if they were up there," said Coach Wilson. "And we have checked the floor each time we have taken the players' bus out. But today I will examine the contents of everyone's duffel bag and the water cooler. I hope you have a good idea of what has happened, young lady!"

The team players slowly came forward to have their duffel bags checked. Their smiles were puzzling to Bree and Nick. The slow process should have made them a bit aggravated with such an inconvenience. Parents were getting out of their cars they had brought to pick up their teens. They were curious to see what was causing the holdup.

The Detective Company sat quietly as the team slowly made their way off the bus. "Well, I didn't discover one tennis ball!" said the coach as he snapped the lid back on the water cooler. "I knew my players would not steal them. I give up!"

"Wait, Coach Wilson," said Hannah. "There is one more place to look."

"Preposterous, young lady," observed the coach. "We have searched every inch of this bus. You cannot see. If you could, you would know there is no other place on this bus to hide 59 tennis balls."

"Did anyone notice that no one was chewing gum as they left the bus?" Hannah asked.

Everyone turned to look at Hannah.

"I may not be able to see, but I could hear them chewing those big wads of gum as we traveled. Then as we neared the school, the chewing had stopped. Did everyone swallow their gum? Check the underside of the players' seats.

You may find your tennis balls."

With a grunt, the coach bent down to look under a seat near the front of the bus and yelled a happy, "Listen up! There are dozens of tennis balls stuck under the seats with that horrible gum!"

The coach stood up to look out the bus windows but all the players had disappeared into cars that had driven away. With a snort, he began gathering tennis balls and happily placed them into the bag that the team manager had left on the bus.

Hannah with Mellow, Nick and Bree walked with Maggie to her car. As Maggie drove them toward their homes, Hannah told about their findings and they all discussed what may have happened.

Hannah shared her insight that when Bree and Nick had told her about the players bobbing up and down in their seats, she thought they may be passing balls back to others so that the balls could be hidden.

When she heard the silence of the players as they finished their ride back to Centerville, she noticed that no longer was anyone chewing gum. If they were not hiding the tennis balls in their duffel bags, she decided the balls must be sticking to the undersides of the seats. Maggie praised Hannah for her good work before they reached her home.

The next afternoon, Hannah stood to report her solution to **The Case of The Vanishing Tennis Balls** to the other members of The Detective Company. They all applauded and cheered when she finished.

The Centerville newspaper carried the story. Coach Wilson had been contacted and told the reporter how his players had played this practical joke because he had gone to such lengths to stress the importance of losing no tennis balls. That the team had planned to surprise him with all 100 balls when they had achieved the disappearance of all the tennis balls.

The news story ended with congratulations to Hannah on solving the case and stated proudly that her success again showed what an important role The Detective Company played for the community of Centerville.

The End